Snow, Ashes

Other Books by Alyson Hagy

Keeneland
Graveyard of the Atlantic
Hardware River
Madonna on Her Back

SNOW, ASHES

Alyson Hagy

Graywolf Press

SAINT PAUL, MINNESOTA

Publication of this volume is made possible in part by a grant provided by the Minnesota State Arts Board, through an appropriation by the Minnesota State Legislature; a grant from the Wells Fargo Foundation Minnesota; and a grant from the National Endowment for the Arts, which believes that a great nation deserves great art. Significant support has also been provided by the Bush Foundation; Target; the McKnight Foundation; and other generous contributions from foundations, corporations, and individuals. To these organizations and individuals we offer our heartfelt thanks.

Published by Graywolf Press
2402 University Avenue, Suite 203
Saint Paul, Minnesota 55114
All rights reserved.

www.graywolfpress.org

Printed in Canada

ISBN 978-1-55597-468-8

2 4 6 8 9 7 5 3 1
First Graywolf Printing, 2007

Library of Congress Control Number: 2006938262

Cover design: www.VetoDesignUSA.com

Cover photograph: Jupiterimages

For Val,
true as the Wyoming wind

A chance to be alone for a chance to be abandoned,
Everything is lost or given.

JAMES GALVIN

Prologue

Trumpet Bell Land & Sheep Company

Baggs, Wyoming

1942

ON THE LAST AFTERNOON OF DOCKING AND BRANDING, Uncle Gene Laury told John Fremont Adams it was time for him to cut a lamb. The men laughed and nodded. They paused to wipe their bloody, shitty fingers on the tails of their wet neckerchiefs. The men believed Adams was big enough now, tall enough to reach the *barrabilak* with his teeth. And he *was* ready. He felt like he'd been ready for a long time. He had a good Baker knife with a four-inch blade. He'd used the knife to notch the ears of some older ewes the year before. He pulled the Baker from his pocket, and Uncle Gene checked the blade but didn't bother to slide it across his oiled whetstone. It was sharp.

Shaggy-haired Francisco lifted a thrashing buck lamb onto the flat-topped docking rail. He pinned the lamb against his hard, smeared belly. He didn't want Adams to get kicked in the face his first time. That would happen soon enough. They'd all been kicked, all been nose-broke, by skittish lambs.

Old Etchepare, the boss herder, talked him through it. First, the step cut—down and out—on the right ear. Then you grabbed the lamb's flabby pink sac. You sliced the end off as fast as you could, squeezing the tiny, pale balls until they could be tugged loose with your teeth. You breathed slow through your nose, and you held the balls soft and hot and easy in your lips, the tendons dangling against your chin while you swiped the lamb's belly with antiseptic. Next came the tail. You pulled it straight and twisted, cut it half through, then twisted it completely off in one more motion. That was the best way to staunch the bleeding. Buck tails got tossed into one pile, ewe tails in another so you'd know how many you had of each. He spat the slick, gristly balls into the metal bucket at his feet. The

5

bucket was nearly full of *barrabilak*. It had been filled many times that day. Later, he'd eat his share of them fried with onion and potato. They all would. He wiped his sticky mouth with his checkered sleeve as the men hi-ohed and clapped.

Another lamb. Old Etch said it was good to start with two. Adams planned how he'd learn to do it fast—under twenty seconds like the finest *artzainak*—as he slit and tugged and spat again. Francisco's brother, Basilio, smiled to show his soiled teeth and tossed Adams a grimy, half-filled *bota*. Adams uncorked the goatskin bag and rinsed his mouth until wine spilled down his neck into his collar. Uncle Gene reset his ruined felt hat on his white brow and pretended not to notice. Uncle Gene wasn't one to exaggerate a mood, but Adams knew he was pleased. Gene had no sons of his own, no children. He'd built the Trumpet Bell piece by piece, wool contract by wool contract. In just a few years, he'd made it into more than a lingering Laury homestead. But he'd made his share of money mistakes, too. The land he managed belonged primarily to his sister Portia and her husband, David Adams, though it never felt that way to Etchepare and the men, or to young Fremont.

He raised a dirty hand in the direction of his uncle. Gene flicked a thumb against his hat brim in response.

Then it was C.D. Hobbs's turn to cut a lamb. Francisco, who liked to startle the smaller boy, shouted at him to step up and take his own knife from the village of Saint Etienne and do his good work. Adams looked at his friend who was dappled with branding paint and sweat. He was sure the attention would make C.D. nervous, even though C.D. knew Francisco and all the men of the Trumpet Bell. C.D. was on the ranch nearly every weekend. He hitched rides out of Baggs with other ranchers, and his mother, who had no husband and was known for her bad habits, didn't seem to care one way or the other. Adams liked C.D.'s company. They were the same age, and they got along fine. But C.D. didn't have a horse of his own, or even a saddle. He had to borrow gear. He helped with the chores as well as he could. Adams's mother said C.D. Hobbs would always find his way in the world because he worked so hard at it. That was easy enough for Adams to believe. As far as he knew, the lives of boys were meant to strike an honest balance. His own brother, Buren, was up at the house right now with his nose in some book from a correspondence course. Buren sure as hell had never docked a lamb. It wasn't something a person had to do.

Francisco planted a lamb on the rail. Old Etchepare urged C.D. forward, muttering slowly above his tobacco-streaked beard just as he had when he showed the boy how to approach the collie, Nina, and her newborn pups. C.D. got through the step cut all right, but when he went for the lamb's sac, the animal's struggle was fierce and seemed to put the falter in him. He stopped. His head wagged as if it were going loose on his neck. Old Etch stepped closer and spoke briefly into his ear. C.D. jerked his knife hand upward from where it hung by his pant leg and finished the job with an awkward, tearing ferocity. The lamb made a strangled, gummy sound, but Francisco held it fast. C.D. Hobbs made no sound at all.

The men hesitated a moment, then cheered when C.D. unclenched his left hand and dropped the nubbin buck tail onto the pile. Francisco laughed his gallant, victorious laugh. But no one gave C.D. the *bota*. They waited for Adams to do that. C.D. sloshed the sour red wine over his sunburned lips, coughed, then pretended to hiccup. The men laughed again as they broke away to their assigned tasks as smoothly as mallards breaking away from a flock in flight. The day was passing. There were lambs and ewes left to muster.

C.D. stood close to Adams, his eyes crinkled shut below his flushed forehead. His chin glistened with mucus and blood. "You see that, Fremont? Cisco picked me a big one. I damn near had to tear his tail off. It ain't easy like it looks."

"No, it's not. Old Etch and Gene's the only ones I ever seen good at it." Adams wiped his hands for about the twelfth time on his denims. The two big swallows of wine he'd taken had only made him thirstier.

"So how'd you like the taste, them raw balls?"

Adams spit into the dirt to keep from smiling. C.D. Hobbs

never knew when to hold back. He always got so excited, so talky. Hobbs wasn't tall or strong, and he sometimes went rabbit when you least expected it, but he generally headed toward the things he liked at a full tilt gallop. "They ain't in the mouth to taste," Adams reminded him. "It's work."

"I was just thinking they'd have to taste like some flavor. They's from lamb, and I know how lamb is flavored. I've eat it enough. Your mother cooks it good."

"So does Basilio."

"Well, yeah, I've eat his, too." C.D. stopped to look at his loose bootlaces. Even those seemed worthy of pride. Behind him, the newly docked lambs cried so hard their ribs flexed. The young animals were stunned by the heat and the grappling. It sometimes took them hours to find their frantic mothers in the packed corrals. "Balls must taste of something," C.D. said.

"But they don't."

C.D. gave another false hiccup. "I'm ready to do it exact right next time."

"Me, too." Adams hadn't realized until then that Hobbs had cut only one buck lamb. Maybe Old Etch and Uncle Gene thought one was enough since it had so flustered the boy. Etch and Gene had a good understanding of people. Uncle Gene was the one who had suggested it was sometimes best to let C.D. Hobbs go on for a while until he got himself unwound into a place where he could stay put.

"We get in on the grub, right?"

"Yeah," said Adams, thinking of the lamb fries and Basilio's peppery mutton stew and fresh sourdough bread. "I'm dead hungry now."

"I can't wait to try again. That'll be all right, won't it, Fremont? Your uncle will let me try again?"

Adams swatted at the fat horse fly chevroned on his thigh. He didn't like it much when C.D. came at him with a plea. It made him tight. "Sure he will. Gene likes cheap help, especially if it don't drink."

"You'll ask him for me? I . . . I don't know if I can say what. . . . Please?"

Adams saw the bright and bottomless worry at the center of C.D.'s eyes. The boy looked like he was about to cry. Adams knew his mother would tell him to pay attention to C.D.'s feelings because good friends didn't add to one another's troubles. His mother would remind him he needed to go easy on the people he liked. "Yeah, sure, I'll take care of it." He tried to ignore the irritation that bit at the back of his neck. "It won't be no problem."

They heard a loud squawk then, a familiar stubborn shriek. Adams's little sister, Charlotte, had apparently put her baby fingers in the hot branding paint again. Adams pulled his hands over his denims, drying them, while C.D. hustled around the chute to where Fred Cosgriff was painting the ranch's $\wedge$ on the lambs, and Charlotte was supposed to be staying out of trouble. Fred Cosgriff doted on Charlotte, but he couldn't always keep a close eye on her. C.D., who didn't have any little ones hanging onto his britches' legs day and night, had a lot of patience with the younger girl. Adams watched C.D. bend down and swing Charlotte up into his skinny arms. His two-year-old sister's golden hair flew above the fence line, tangling around the meadowlark feathers she'd woven into a flapping crown. He heard C.D. say something that made Charlotte laugh. C.D. was also good at that, getting Charlotte to laugh. He would be able to convince Charlotte that her job was to keep Nina's new pups away from the camp stove while the older dogs, Nina and Pat and Nola and Bill, leaped in and out of the corrals, adding their scolding barks to the gruff shouts of the men.

Adams studied the shadows that had begun to fold into the veils of hoof-stirred dust that hung over the corrals. If there was moisture in the air, he couldn't taste it. He tasted only the iron of his fatigue and the stirred breeze that was flavored with the vinegars of vitriol and piss. Hundreds of lambs and ewes surged into the rough fence boards of the corrals, bucking and scraping their bodies against confinement. Again and again, they wheeled and broke like cream-finned fish in search of open water. He felt the quick way they moved in the quickness of his blood. In a few days, two thousand of them, bleating and bankrolled and shit-crusted, would make their way toward summer pasture in the Sierra Madres. He wouldn't be going with them.

Although he was ten, Adams wasn't considered old enough to tend herd in the mountains. He'd been put in charge of the bucks and dry ewes that would pasture close to home instead, and he would divide those duties with Blue Pete Tosh, the aging Scot who'd lost his night vision and could no longer sight a coyote's rib cage with his rifle. Adams was disappointed, but Uncle Gene said he should be proud. Caring for bucks was the start, a step up the staircase. Old Etchepare said it was his first chance to be *gizona,* and that word meant something to him. Old Etch was Basque and had spent thirty years herding sheep in the basin. He was chief of them all.

But there would be slashing rainstorms in the mountains. And prowling coyotes. Maybe even rustlers. There would be more trouble than Tito and Albert and Etch and Francisco could handle, he just knew it. They would need him.

He took his straw hat from his head and looked at the bold red uplift of Bell Butte, the way its western face splintered against the setting sun. He didn't hear Old Etchepare until the boss herder placed a hard, square hand upon his shoulder.

"*Berhala,* young one. You and the boy do good today. *Mendiak* will wait for you one more year. All thing come soon enough."

Adams nodded. He knew he should keep Old Etch's advice as close to his chest as a medicine pouch. But he wasn't going to hide his disappointment. "I know what to do in the mountains. I could help out."

The herder squeezed the lean muscle of Adams's shoulder until Adams flinched, then he grinned around his gapped, yellow teeth. His breath, as always, was sweet with the dark syrups he mixed into his tobacco. "You have *bihotza,* big heart for to protect the herd. I know this. I see it with your friend, who have a different heart from you, more like what beats in the chest of *San Juan del Desierto.* You watch over that boy.

He watch what cannot be seen with a tall man's eye. You take care of him."

"C.D. and me get along all right. But he don't need to go into the Madres like I want to." Adams rubbed at a bug bite on his face. He knew better than to stare too hard at Old Etchepare. "I know how to take care of the sheep."

The old man did not laugh at him, or soften his declaration in any way. "You have *bihotza,* which is good. I admire the heart. But sometime more is needed to make the best of life. This what we tell people of my land—strong or not so strong, rich men or *penitentes,* whoever hear the words. Maybe you listen, also. You must take care. The true *gizona,* we say, does not pray for his testing until he knows he is ready."

Trumpet Bell Land & Sheep Company

Baggs, Wyoming

1995

C.D. HOBBS RETURNED TO THE UNHEATED ROOM IN the machine shed sometime in January. It was long after dark, wind blowing in from the north and west, so his old friend Fremont Adams didn't hear him arrive. The dogs yipped their high-ground warnings, however. That commotion nudged Adams to rise from his chair by the stove, put on his sheepskin coat, his hat, grab at his shotgun. The gun was a boastful habit, and he knew it. He lived too far from good water to worry about lions. He no longer kept enough stock to interest serious coyotes. Few creatures cared to visit his place.

He checked the barn and the horses. The two younger dogs joined him from their rag pallets under the porch, both of them more interested in the beef-stew scent of his pant legs than whatever intrusion or fantasy had set them off. But when he circled behind the barn to patrol the locked fuel tanks, he realized what he was up against. The third dog, a hip-worn collie-cross he called Rain, was standing near the corner of the machine shed, tail stiff, ears up. It was a thing he did only for Hobbs, this naked hope for an invitation. Adams looked over each shoulder into the black aisles of his ranch yard for the blunt, stalled nose of a truck, though he didn't expect to see one. C.D. Hobbs never came with a truck or anything that could be called a possession. He came with the clothes on his back.

Adams breathed through the thick weave of his pulse. Hobbs. Again. His return likely meant trouble. Care and trouble.

The shotgun hung from his hand as he crossed toward the shed. He should greet the man and make sure he had blankets. Invite him to breakfast. He tried to remember what was stored in the small, cold room that was located behind the tractors and the ditcher and the swather. A canvas cot, he was nearly sure about that. And maybe some buckets of sealer compound. He found he couldn't bring the exact litter of the room to mind.

When he got to where Rain had set up his silent courtship, Adams slowed his deliberate march. He prodded himself to approach the skewed yellow door that had once hung in his parents' bedroom, but he couldn't make himself knock on it. He tightened the knuckles of his left hand as he imagined smiling into C.D.'s face. What would he say this time? *Hello, C.D. What the hell brings you here?* No matter how welcoming he might pretend to be, he knew he'd end up scanning for empty bottles or the sloe-eyed stare that came with Hobbs's kind of pills. He told himself it would be better for him and Hobbs to do what they had always done before—see what they saw when they saw it. Acknowledgment wasn't part of the debt they managed between them.

He made his way back to his unlit porch. Rain remained on watch, believing his patience would be rewarded, if not on this frigid night, then on another just like it. He would be allowed to share Hobbs's cot. For the dog it was enough. Adams didn't wonder at the animal's devotion to a man it hadn't seen in years. He knew Rain was a fool, though he'd trained him to be better. Dogs and men had their flaws. He stripped off his stiffened coat and hat, placed the gun hard on its rack. This wasn't the time to brood upon what one man owed another man, what any creature believed it was worth. Such thoughts belonged to morning. Certain of that, Adams carefully banked the stove fire. He worked his aching feet free of his boots and settled into his chair, open-eyed, until the earliest moment he could call dawn.

The phone rang before he boiled up his first cup of coffee. It would be Buren. It was always Buren. The only blessing was the twenty-five miles of phone line that spared him the candied smells of his brother's bourbon and hair oil.

"You're slow today." The voice was loud, raised by leaping vowels. "Usually shut me up after two or three rings."

Adams gave no answer. He spat into the stained basin of his kitchen sink instead.

"If I thought you still cared about working, I'd guess you were outside moving hay or rebuilding one of your monumental engines. Not able to hear the damn phone."

"It's five in the morning, Buren."

"Yes, yes, a sunrise not to be missed. But I know you haven't been sleeping. We share that curse, you'll remember."

"I've got a woman here."

The voice wheezed with pleasure for several breaths before it regained its bullying poise. "No, you haven't. I know every willing female from here to Hanna. Not one of them lacks that much self-respect, drunk or sober. Especially on a Tuesday. But the joke is a good one. I admire a good joke."

Adams poured his coffee, sloshing it across the face of his wristwatch. The dogs, except Rain, were scrabbling hard at the door, wanting in out of the cold. They'd heard the less forbidding notes of his voice.

"I called about some books. You'll come to town in a day or two?"

"Maybe."

"I thought you might bring me a treat. Not that I don't want to come out, but your road and my Buick. . . ."

"Are pieces of shit. Tell me what you need. I'll get them to you sometime."

Buren was a lawyer who'd retired to the tiny town of Baggs after years of conniving with various governors in the state capitol of Cheyenne. His current passion was the renovation of a nineteenth-century house that had once been a brothel, once a home to circuit-riding Presbyterians and their dry biscuits. Buren claimed to despise the hardpan ranch he'd grown up on. He still complained to Adams about the blat of its sheep, its tinged and bitter water, the dust that shrouded its sills. But he seemed to thrive on the ranch's reputation, especially those worn threads of reputation that so cocooned his younger brother. Buren was forever raiding the small, leather-bound library

assembled by their parents—the ledgers, the receipts, the boxed
diaries kept by the young women of the family before they married. He claimed to be writing a book, though he refused to tell
Adams what the book was about. Adams suspected Buren was
merely doing everything he could to keep his schoolmarmish
mind in balance. Drink and redecoration wouldn't be enough.

"I'd like the green volumes on the second shelf. To the left
of the door, please. Both of them."

He always did it that way, described the books by color and
location as if Adams couldn't read the titles stamped on the
flaking spines as well as he could. Adams was about to hang
up the phone, his tolerance for insult reached, when he remembered. "Hobbs is back. I haven't seen him yet, but he's here."

There was a rare moment of silence before Buren launched
his response. *"Her grief moves hitherward like an angry sea."*

Adams resisted the obvious question. Sipped his coffee.

"Medea," Buren purred. "One of the plays you brought
to me last month. It's a Greek tragedy in which C.D. Hobbs
might gladly take a part if he were that sort of vengeful man,
which I know you believe he is not. Still, I think of our sister Charlotte." He paused as if he expected Adams to fill the
chasms around that name. Adams didn't oblige. "How long
has it been since he tried to hold a job with you? Five years?
And three years before that? He ended up strapped to a bug-
house bed both times, but I'll wager you're going to try to take
care of him again. His madness always manages to draw you
in. Is it because he's never given up on you?"

Adams closed his eyes as his ears filled with a battery roar he
hadn't allowed himself to hear in a long time. It was the sound
of howitzers hurling thunder and smoke at the black rock of
Korea. He felt the splintering of a thousand past concussions
along the eroded surfaces of his knees. He smelled the smell
of bad things burning. "I've never known C.D. to give up
on much of anything. He was always the other way, the loyal
kind, a hanger-on. He's been like that since we were boys. It's
just like you to think loyalty is a waste of time." Adams rushed

through the verbal stab he'd aimed at his brother. He felt now what he hadn't allowed himself to feel during the night, a sheath of responsibility so tight it made his words taste heated in his mouth. "I'll give him work, Buren, if he's able. And I'll keep him clear of you and your pissant sensitivities."

He dropped the receiver into its cradle. Then he wiped up the coffee he'd spilled with a rag made from the sleeve of one of his old flannel shirts. He listened for the dogs, but he could no longer hear them. They had happily abandoned him for the daylight that was levering itself over Bell Butte and the calicoed roofs of his ranch.

Later that morning Adams opened the porch door to see Hobbs waiting for him like a delivered parcel.

"H-hello, Fremont. D-didn't want to disturb you, knocking on the door after dark like . . ."

". . . like bad news." Adams tried a smile.

"Sorry if it weren't the proper thing. I knew where to bunk."

"It's all dandy and fine," Adams said. "The dogs got you figured better than I do. They knew the score. Why don't you come on in?"

"You don't mind?" Always that question, brief and coiled. This time it was accompanied by a depleted squeeze of the blue eyes.

"Nobody's crowded with company around here." Adams gazed at the unpainted lathe that roofed his porch, its knots and gaps. Then he extended his right hand toward Hobbs, and they shook. Adams tried to ignore the flush of blood that surged across his face. He always felt more on edge when Hobbs was around, sharper about some things but also needled with worry. Even when things were going well, the two of them had a way of complicating each other. "I could use some help if you're willing."

"Th-thank you so v-very. . . . I prayed th-that. . . ." Hobbs's voice narrowed into a wordless creak. He drew his neck down

into his collar in a kind of ranch hand's bow, then composed
himself enough to speak. "I prayed to work on the Trumpet
Bell again. Your family has always b-b-been good to me."

It was the first fresh lie to fall between them. Adams felt something like a screw turn deep in his belly, but he said nothing.

Adams made their first breakfast together, and Hobbs cleaned
up, putting pots in cupboards where they didn't belong just as
he always had. Adams noticed that Hobbs had changed some
since they'd last seen each other. He still had the tremor in his
left hand. And his right ear was still no more than a remnant
stalk of burned and twisted skin. Seeing the old burns made
Adams want to scratch at the side of his own head. He'd never
gotten used to Hobbs's wounds. Now, however, there were new
pads of flesh above and below Hobbs's belt buckle. Age had
drawn whatever was still malleable in him toward the place
below his ribs and heart. His face remained familiar—Adams
would have known him anywhere—yet it wasn't the same. It
was younger and fresher around the blue filament eyes, if that
was possible in a man who'd worked on ranches and oil rigs
every moment he'd had his health.

After breakfast, they convened in the parlor where they considered the vagaries of the weather.

"Do you b-believe it'll snow?" Hobbs asked. "Looks like
you could use more snow."

Adams said he thought it would snow before the end of the
week.

"Still lose your electric out here during a g-good storm?"
Hobbs's selected memories of the Trumpet Bell were so pleas-
ant, so eager, they caused his face to shine with sweat.

Adams said, "I keep plenty of candles." He could feel how
right it was that they both knew the choruses of ranch life.
Each note. Every refrain. The two of them were safe, even after
fifty years, in the haltered pleasures of those habits.

As safe, Adams thought, as they could ever be.

Adams folded his body into the false leather recliner that
was angled to catch heat from the stove. Hobbs perched him-

self on the straight-backed desk chair that had been made by
Blue Pete Tosh after he went completely blind. Neither of them
used the cabbage-rose settee that faced the windows to the
west. They could have viewed two thousand of the Trumpet
Bell's thirty-six thousand acres from the settee, but it was left
empty, cleared of books and the thin pages of the *Rawlins
Daily Times*. The settee was reserved for company, should they
ever have any.

"I c-c-can't quite believe in it all," Hobbs said. "Things look
the same, but they ain't. This house smells the s-same, but it
can't be." Adams watched Hobbs stroke the surface of the
walnut writing desk with the oily edge of his palm. It was a
solemn, distracted thing Adams's mother had done while she
labored to balance the ranch accounts at that very same desk.

"I don't know," Adams said. "I been here so long it all
seems logjammed to me. I might have to use my imagination to
keep us busy."

Hobbs continued to buff the desktop. Adams wondered
if Hobbs was aware of what he was doing. Maybe he'd just
absorbed the gesture like he'd absorbed so many of the other
behaviors—good and bad—he'd witnessed on the Trumpet Bell.

"Do what you must, Fremont. Make your decisions count."
The declaration was a surprise. And it came toward Adams in a
voice that wasn't Hobbs's. There was no hesitation, no stutter.
Adams heard his mother's particular and gentle lilt in Hobbs's
words, the tune of a voice that had been silent for more than
thirty years. He checked to make sure his mouth wasn't hanging open. He shut, then reopened his eyes. It was too early
in Hobbs's visit to get spooked; he told himself that. Hobbs
had always been a kind of mockingbird. It was only natural—
wasn't it?—that he could recall every pose and posture of the
Adams clan, heartening or not.

"Yes, ma'am," he said, out of reflex. "You know I will."

The next morning, after the horses had been turned out and
breakfast had been scraped off the gold-trimmed plates from
the 1964 World's Fair, Hobbs asked for the keys to the truck.

"What for?" Adams assumed Hobbs had groceries in mind. They'd spent the day before wandering the fence lines and creek beds of the Trumpet Bell's deeded land. But neither of them had given much thought to supplies.

"Wednesday." Hobbs's eyes twitched into a steady series of blinks. "I believe it's W-wednesday. I still get lost on that sometimes. Don't you ride Mesa ditch on a Wednesday?"

Adams hadn't told Hobbs that he was no longer a manager for the water conservation district. He'd been able to deflect Hobbs's early questions about sheep by implying his spring ewes were scheduled to ship in. But Adams hadn't owned sheep in four years. These days the only way he could enjoy their good, lanolin stink was after a hard rain. And this past summer, after more than twenty years of service, the water board had given him the boot. They wanted somebody with more irrigated land to his name, more spark. Adams had left the position without a word, although Buren had been wry, even caustic, on his behalf. Buren had planted a large sign in his front yard in Baggs that read *Et tu, Compton,* a reference to the backstabbing board president.

But Adams still had all his gate keys, for god's sake, the whole heavy ring of them. What difference would an explanation of his forced retirement make? Hobbs hadn't asked for a pissed-off update of Adams's life. He hadn't asked about losses or failures. He'd just asked to ride a damn ditch.

"All right. Let's do it," Adams said. "I'll show you how bad the spread of leafy spurge has got."

They drove in by way of Cheet Tuttle's leased pastureland. The sky over the snow-crowned Sierra Madres was blockaded by a fleet of smooth-sailing clouds. The morning sunlight surged ahead of the clouds like a rising silver tide. At the pasture gate, tire tracks from the new district manager's truck had congealed into ochre braids of soil. Adams resisted the urge to erase every trace of his replacement with his spinning tires. Hobbs looked at the tracks as though he ought to recognize them, then he stepped out of the truck to untangle the gate's iron hook and chain.

The conservation district had thoroughly renovated First Mesa since Hobbs's last stay in the valley. As they drove along the clean, graded berm that sheltered the main irrigation ditch, Hobbs couldn't contain his enthusiasm. Several times he signaled Adams to stop. He got out of the truck and ambled the sloped clay banks while a steady, icy wind teased at his coat collar. He pinched various grades of gravel between his fingers. He pushed his salted black cap above his hairline in admiration of the unchoked plumes and weirs. Dozens of fallen cottonwoods had been dragged clear and cut up for firewood. Several tons of riprap had been dumped into the curves of the ditch to reduce summer erosion when the water was high. They had never had the money to upgrade this ditch, the two of them. They'd had only their manpower, a tandem gift as scavengers, to keep the water flowing as well as they could.

"You done good out here," Hobbs said.

Adams responded with a plastic smile.

He remembered Hobbs using a tricycle-wheeled tractor to shove the rusted body of a 1927 Reo truck into a steep corner of that very ditch. In the old days they'd used junk—anything they could find—to stabilize those cutbanks. But these were better times. They drove on across young Gil Gunderson's parcel and the land Annie Els had just sold to a realtor out of Denver. Adams, massaging the clutch of his Ford pickup, watched Hobbs leap onto the wing of a slide gate near Dutch Joe Draw, the sky bird empty above him. He thought about how Hobbs had jury-rigged that very gate through thankless years of drought and low pay. God damn, they'd made a whole lot of something out of nothing in those days. They could have been real engineers. They could have gone to college, flung up dams in Arizona or Egypt or anywhere they pleased. If things had been just a little different, he and C.D. Hobbs might not have spent a thousand dusk hours cleaning thistle and beaver bone from sorry ditches carrying water to sorrier fields.

Adams finessed the truck to a halt. He was opposite the cone-roofed gauge house he and a neighbor's son had built two years before. He could see new bullet holes in the siding, up to a dozen of them. The culprits were usually local joy riders or drunk, out-of-state elk hunters who got lost looking for access to Battle Mountain. But sometimes the target practice was more thematic. Charles McNamee, or somebody who worked for him, had blasted the lock off the gauge house twice because they'd been sure the Bar Diamond D outfit upstream was stealing their precious acre-feet of water. Adams had smoothed those ruffled rancher feathers many times during his twenty years of irrigation work, but the quarrels remained. Somebody had pumped lead into his gauge house.

He took his keys from the truck's ignition, feeling righteous and peeved and blood hot before he realized the gauge house was no longer his responsibility. He paused a second before he let the feelings run on just the same. It had been a long while since he'd owned a good aggravation. If Hobbs was going to have a high time surveying the old territory, then so was he. He looked for C.D. and saw him sidling off the small Dutch Joe dam. Hobbs loved tasks. He always had. He could find joy in a bent nail as long as it was within reach of a hammer. Adams waved him back.

"Why don't you check the diversion? See it's clear."

Hobbs nodded.

Then Adams opened the padlock and the gauge-house door and saw that the meters and power line to the solar cell were intact. He flicked the test switch to make sure. Up close the bullet holes didn't appear so fresh. There were collars of rust where the paint had been blasted away. The holes had been made after the first of September; he was god damn sure of that. He wouldn't have missed them when he was still on the job.

He had been good at irrigating. Good at more than a few things, once. He wished he didn't have to remind himself of that.

He banged the gauge-house door shut and hip-chucked it until the warped latch fit over the U-bolt. The hinges needed to be replaced—that was a problem for the new manager. He looked for Hobbs again, found him on the narrow catwalk of the dam. *Hold on*, Hobbs signaled. *Almost done.* He had spread his spindly jean-clad legs and was gripping the red-painted hand wheel that regulated the flow of water during irrigation season. His elbows were at the level of his mismatched ears.

There was nothing below the guillotine gate but ice and defeated leaves, the ditches were empty, but Hobbs always had to handle a thing to see how it worked, *if* it was working. He was torquing the wheel to make sure the gears were properly greased for cold weather. Yet the motions he made pincered Adams in a vivid, unsought memory: C.D. Hobbs at fifteen or sixteen, child of a mother with no gumption, a father never mentioned, forging the raging snowmelt of Savery Creek on his own. He held a panicked, bawling lamb in his arms; his elbows were exactly that high. The fast water festooned his shoulders like lace.

Adams squeezed his eyes shut. Was it a lamb Hobbs had carried to safety through the flood that day or a piece of camping equipment they'd forgotten during a foolish fishing trip to the other side? Suddenly, he couldn't be sure. So much time had passed, so many unpleasant memories had been culled and starved. He turned his face away from the beckoning sun, hoping to corral the restlessness that was too often in his head these days. He thought back. He tried to put the pieces together in a way that would satisfy him. Tried to remember. But he couldn't recall the exact circumstances of that long-ago adventure on Savery Creek. He cursed himself as he gimped back to the Ford, his feet paining him as they always did in winter. What good was a good memory you couldn't trust? And what did it mean—for himself, for his companion—if he could no longer reconstruct C.D. Hobbs's one sure moment among the brave?

Hobbs thought the first thing they should do was overhaul the smaller of the ranch's two tractors. Adams had postponed the task because he couldn't lift the engine block alone and, as Buren so often reminded him, he could no longer afford to hire help. But Hobbs's presence had become a kind of sputtering inspiration.

It took most of an afternoon to clear a proper space in the

machine shed. Then they had to erect the tripod and re-rig the rusty block and tackle. The winter sky lapped at the stone-dark edges of a few clouds, but the temperature was mild enough to work bare-handed, and the steady sunlight lured a small band of sparrows into the ranch yard to peck for seeds. When Adams barked the knuckles of both hands trying to seat the tractor engine in the cradle, his loud string of curses led Hobbs to ease into a rare curse of his own. "Shit," he said, sounding remarkably like his watery-eyed friend. "Damn it to h-hell, and shit."

"You got that right," Adams said, licking at his own blood. "Amen."

When Hobbs sluiced himself with oil as he was trying to drain the engine, Adams led both of them into hoarse laughter. A fresh sense of accomplishment began to simmer between them. They were stockmen who still knew how to stay one step ahead of the game. Adams watched Hobbs amble toward the barn to retrieve a tool, and he couldn't help but notice how efficiently the other man carried himself. His shoulders were slouched, but his arms were corded and strong. He walked like a man who knew how to pace himself for a long haul down an unkept road. It was the way Old Etchepare had walked.

Adams's enthusiasm didn't wane even as the sunlight did. "A good day like this," he said, "just about deserves a party."

Hobbs glanced up from the dusty tangle of the tractor's ignition wires. His forehead looked as if it had been tattooed with grease.

"What do you say to a tall drink by the hot stove?" Adams continued. "Along with a few good-tasting cigarettes."

Hobbs hesitated. "D-don't know, Fremont. I been away from the drinking. D-doctors prefer me that way."

Adams wanted to kick himself. Hobbs hadn't said a single word about hospitals or medication since he'd returned, and Adams had been afraid to ask. But here he was—stepping right into the shit hole.

"How about you watch me empty a glass or two then?" He tried to make his request sound like a joke. "No pressure. We'll just talk or not talk. Maybe daydream our way into some plans for this place."

"P-plans. I like plans," Hobbs said, prying his thin lips into a smile. "I been thinking about some of those on my own."

"Okay. All right. We'll have a little celebration after dinner." Adams found that it was suddenly difficult for him to focus on the syllables of Hobbs's words. His ears were thick with the current of a new momentum. He and Hobbs were onto something. He and the old boy were actually on a roll. He could feel the good speed of it in his veins.

Hobbs returned from gathering and feeding the horses at exactly 7 p.m. He removed his brown hunting cap and hung it with his quilted vest in the mudroom. Adams thought his friend was on the verge of some breed of laughter as he shooed the dogs back into the night, but Hobbs didn't make any human noise. The dogs all followed him now, their marbled eyes wide with expectation. Both men avoided words until Hobbs began to scrub his hands at the sink as if for a meal. "I think," he said, "I think my hands are very clean." He spoke at a low volume, as if his throat had become raw and sore.

Adams had already inaugurated the scotch, just a small glass, so he offered Hobbs a mug of reheated coffee along with a paper napkin and a spoon. He took the lidded sugar bowl from its place on top of the refrigerator and watched as Hobbs stirred a single spoonful of sugar into his mug. Then he went back to the stove where he was trying to heat oil in a blackened pot for popcorn. He heard Hobbs reach for the glass jar of corn, purchased from the Stage Stop in Baggs. When he checked over his shoulder, Hobbs was peering at the jar's labels as if he was trying to make the tiny-lettered sentences agree with him.

They'd had poached eggs for breakfast. The kitchen still smelled of bacon and Tabasco. "This," Adams said, as the oil in the pot smoked and spat, "you'd think was easier than the poaching of hen's eggs, but it's not."

"You done a good job with the eggs," Hobbs said, still

throaty. "I-I can't keep the yellow part separate, have to pour on the ketchup to cover my mistake."

"It's nothing but luck and patience."

"Your mother said it took the right tool. She had a spatula with a wood handle on it. M-maybe we should get one like that."

Adams laughed, adding an even layer of corn to the black bottom of the pot. "Basilio did that up at summer camp. You remember how he cooked everything with that one knife and the spatula he never washed? Wore them stuck through his belt loops when he needed his hands free."

"Made the biscuits dirt-colored," Hobbs said. "They still tasted g-good as long as he had salt. To me, anyway."

Adams laughed again at Hobbs's idea of tasty food. Preferences were all right with him. How else did you tell one man from another? Some nights, such as this one, *should* be different from all the rest, just as men should be different from one another. That was his preference for the moment. He swirled the pot over the steady blue flame of the gas burner, barely touching the pot handles with his fingertips to keep from getting burned. He jumped when the first corn kernels exploded, his heels slipping upward in his boots. He was never quite ready for that sound.

Hobbs was standing at the center of the parlor's oval braided rug when Adams entered with a bowl of popcorn in one hand, the now buttery swirl of scotch in the other. Hobbs was standing, not sitting, and he hadn't lit his cigarette. He wasn't pacing, but he looked spring-wound to do something of the sort. His collarbones bowed forward under the light and dark fabrics of his layered shirts. His left hand swung outward from his hip and vibrated with its untransmittable palsy. The shaking was as bad as Adams had ever seen it. Hobbs faced the framed, unglassed picture that hung above the cabbage-rose settee, a pasteboard reproduction of Thomas Moran's painting of the Tetons. Adams's father had cherished that picture as a panorama of grandeur where he had none.

Adams saw how he'd drawn his own clear line across the

room. His recliner, the woodstove, and the television were in a tight triangle of space near the door. The rest of it—the towers of books and ledgers, his mother's proud and settled furniture, the filing cabinet stuffed with lease records and receipts, the unused computer, the undusted lamps, the spiraling rug—floated free of his private island. He wondered how Hobbs could look so lost in a room that crowded and small.

"Let's eat while it's hot," he said. "I've done a sloppy job with the buttering as it is."

Hobbs shifted his weight from one leg to the other, jittery, but he went to his straight-backed chair and sat. He looked across the room in a way that exposed the pale skin of his throat. The slick, ropey scars below his ear were not visible. He didn't speak. Adams thought of how he'd imagined these moments: friendly talk, an hour or two of fellowship followed by sleep and long, questing dreams ushered in by the scotch. He'd had his hopes. But something had tied a sudden, unslippable knot inside Hobbs. He'd seen it before. Oh, he had. Such knots could be untied, if the people around Hobbs were careful. He believed he was willing to be careful.

"Here's to good times," he said, offering a spontaneous toast with his glass. He realized too late that he'd forgotten to make sure Hobbs's coffee mug was near at hand—he couldn't see it on the desk—and he'd spoken, even raised his own glass, while displaying the bowl of popcorn as if he were a restaurant waiter burdened by haste and false cheer. He stepped forward and put the heavy, steaming bowl on top of the blind box of the television. He tried again. "Good days ahead." But Hobbs didn't respond except to lower his shaved chin until his eyes no longer reflected the distant kitchen light. Adams wondered if those eyes were splintering with panic. There was that feeling in the air. Maybe he should have allowed the dogs to come inside. Or asked Hobbs to refill the stove with wood, gotten him to participate in that way. Maybe if he'd done one thing different.

"Well, if you aren't hungry after that poor show of a stew I put on for dinner, I don't need the extra calories any more than you do. Probably needs more salt on it, anyway, like those biscuits." He waved at the popcorn. Slurped at his drink a little, trying to convey a casual sloppiness he didn't feel. Hobbs didn't move. Adams stood silent for some time, waiting, and then he began to talk as if to himself. It was the kind of stubborn rehearsal often witnessed by the high-ceilinged parlor when he was the only one in it.

"It might help us both, C.D., if you gave me a reason for quitting on me here. I thought we were on some sort of track until a minute ago. We had a good day today. I had a fine feeling. I'd rather not waste this kind of time down the road."

He was suddenly angry, and he wanted to cow Hobbs with the noise of that anger. He knew if he kept himself mad he'd be able to weld a heavy hatch over his growing fear.

"What's the deal with you, really? Why can't you come inside and eat a snack with me like a normal man? We have one high minute going on about eggs, then you balk. And why don't you sleep in this house at night? It's not like I said you couldn't. You don't have to stay out there like one of the damn dogs." He watched Hobbs's chest and shoulders absorb the punching flurry of his questions. He was shocked, dizzied even, by how quickly he'd unleashed his forbidden feelings. His jaw muscles had become knots. His hands were like mallets. He'd meant to keep the past behind them. He'd meant to be patient and cautious, not blame Hobbs for anything. But a powerful, rekindled fury was hurling him backwards, back toward the man he'd sworn he'd never be again.

Hobbs tried an explanation. "The d-dogs . . . I like the d-dogs. And . . . and she said to do it this way. Sh-she said."

She? That response, with its brackets of pleading, inflamed Adams even more. She? How dare he. How dare C.D. Hobbs skulk his way back onto this ranch, back into Adams's own life, and mewl out a mention of Charlotte, his estranged sister. They *were not* going to discuss Charlotte. No one was going to drag her back into this house like the dead carcass she was.

"Don't bring up my sister. I got nothing to say about her. This is about you and me. What I see is you coming back—

again—but being afraid to make something of the situation. I try to make things different for us, and you won't let me. So why don't you tell me why the hell you're here? I want to know what I'm supposed to *do*."

Hobbs gave a flat-browed look as though Adams had just answered his own questions. He said, "It's not gonna be like it has been," then he began to polish the top of the walnut desk with his hand, rubbing circles inside of circles. Adams turned toward the two eight-paned windows with their vista of Powder Rim. There was no night sky to be seen, no flaw in the tight-woven skirts of the dark. Wind sifted past the high corners of his house, hissing like sand.

"Do you hear loud talking in your head again, C.D? Is it like . . . the hospital times?" Forming those words broke something flintlike loose from behind his tongue, an erosion below the sure sounds of his words.

"No. Uh-uh." Hobbs's voice was soft, but clear. "I don't *hear* what's visiting me. I-I just feel it sometimes. It's mostly all feeling, Fremont, if you want the truth. But I know what you're saying. You say it every time we g-get together, it's your job. Recognize recognize recognize recognize. That's your part. I have to . . . I do the managing. I-I'm not afraid of nothing, though. I'd rather you didn't say I was the one afraid."

Adams flinched, then drove a shaky hand through his unwashed hair. He tasted a bitterness in his mouth unstaunched by the scotch. "What else I got to go on?"

"I'm just . . . here. That's all it is right n-now."

Hobbs stood up then, bojangled and released. He eased around Adams who lifted his smeared glass to his lips as the man passed by. What could he do but toast old mistakes and their results? He'd gotten exactly what he deserved. He'd toppled all the skeletons right out of the closet. Korea. Charlotte. Hospitals. The failed and useless ranch. And he'd strangled his own best intentions as if they were infant children.

He listened to the scrapes and motions of Rain and the other dogs as Hobbs met them at the porch door, the hasty greetings there. Why hadn't he been able to say what he'd planned to say ever since they'd both gone up to their elbows in the slick guts of the tractor? *We used to be good together. We can still be good.* Instead, he'd ruined his chance. His dreams wouldn't be slow and riverlike tonight, not now. They would be hard and frescoed inside his skull. He tasted the thick slab of intruding cold as the door closed behind Hobbs and the dogs. He listened as his house fell silent except for the collapse of the stove's fading fire.

The next morning Hobbs was gone with both horses. Adams wasn't surprised. He had expected a reaction to his stupid tantrum. But he kept himself from visiting Hobbs's room to see if the bedroll and change of clothes had also disappeared because he knew he wasn't ready for that disappointment. The horses were unshod and cold-backed from neglect, yet he trusted Hobbs. Hobbs wouldn't abuse an animal no matter how bad things got.

He stayed busy patching a leak in a wagon tire because it afforded him a choreography that kept him outdoors. The dawn had been swept clean by a quick, nagging breeze. He fixed an eye on the scrubbed hearth of the horizon as the light warmed itself from pebble gray to the color of a grouse's egg, and he thought about what he'd do if he were C.D. Hobbs, wanted and unwanted, trying to live with another old man who didn't know his future.

If he were choosing an escape route, he'd pack up food and water and ride a horse west into Windmill Draw. He'd follow Willow Creek into the vast nothing of Sand Creek, then turn south onto the old, unfenced grazing route used by every sheep man in the region during the years before the Taylor Grazing Act. At some point he'd pause and recall bouncing on the buckboard of Old Etchepare's bright green sheep wagon as they drove a thousand dirty Rambouillet asses down the split, waterless braid of Sand Creek. He'd listen for the militant bark of dogs and remember how incessantly the flimsy lambs had butted at their mothers' shorn flanks for milk. He'd try to spot the driftwood-colored vault of his house from the height

of Antler Knob. Then he'd ride over the rusty spur of Skull
Creek Rim toward the empty clarity of the mountains where
he'd raise a canvas tent and heat it with a tin-sided stove. He
would remember the country and all the uses it once had for
him. What he'd do after that he didn't know. It didn't seem important to finish the journey, just to start it.

He polished this imaginary ride away from his guilt for
many hours.

Hobbs was back by late afternoon. He was astride the age-
bleached roan. The sorrel trailed behind wearing a cinched but
empty packsaddle. Hobbs had never been a natural on horse-
back, not like Adams or his sister Charlotte. His posture was all
elbows and knees. But both horses were sound, and their liquid
eyes held the disinterest of the adequately fed and watered.
Adams took the reins to the roan as Hobbs clambered off.

"Here we are. Blowed right back to where we started."
Hobbs grinned around his overlapped front teeth. "I should
have known that's how it would end, but you can't tell exactly
what any day might bring to you because if you could you'd be
G-god or dead."

"They give you any trouble?" Adams asked. He realized
that despite the white burn of relief he felt at seeing Hobbs, he
wasn't ready to face him. Not yet. "This one has a hard mouth
and a harder head. I haven't ridden them like they need."

"They did good, considering. They was working real smooth
by the time we got to Barrel Springs, even when a big pump
truck come blasting by. I wondered if I knew the driver, but he
got past me too quick."

Adams was certain Hobbs didn't know the truck driver.
Hobbs hadn't worked the Barrel Springs oil field for twenty
years.

"This gelding tongues the bit more than he should. I'd say
he needs his teeth filed. I seen that done once. Animal doctor
from Laramie that Charlotte called. She was good with animals. Real careful about things like that." He gave the roan a
rub across the muzzle with the back of his hand. "I was thinking to take them over to Robber's Gulch for the exercise, see

the buffalo jump that's out that way. I hadn't been there for a long time."

Adams filtered some air through his nose. Stalled. He hadn't seen Hobbs parade after an impulse since the days of Charlotte and only then because he was properly coaxed. Now he'd said her name and talked about her like he expected to see her at Sunday dinner. Why was C.D. putting Charlotte back into the picture? And how had he gotten all the way to Robber's Gulch? The Gulch was a pure seventeen miles southwest of the Trumpet Bell as the falcon flew. Hobbs would have needed to leave the ranch right after their standoff over the popcorn to get there and back.

"We didn't make it, though." Hobbs no longer grinned or showed any lip at all as he talked to the broad side of the sorrel. The packsaddle, which he was beginning to unlash, had been nicely wiped and oiled. "We stopped short. I put up at the old cattle shed by the crossroads when the wind got to deviling the dust. Tried again at dawn, but finally had to reverse the wagon train."

He might have been counting in Greek as much sense as the inflections of his voice made, though his hands worked carefully, step by step, easy on the mare. He seemed to be on some kind of teeter-totter. Clear, then unclear. Focused, then faltering. Adams loosened the cinch on the roan gelding and thought about Robber's Gulch. There were some old hunting blinds out that way, the work of Ute Indians or sheep men, nobody much cared to distinguish. Uncle Gene had shown them quite a few Indian pictures in that area, some of them painted in colors, some of them chipped right into the overhanging bellies of sandstone with sharp-pointed rocks. In one place a wiseass herdsman had added big-tit *chiquitas* to some of the scenes, but many of the pictures were untouched. Like they spooked even the wiseasses. Old Etchepare, who had handled sheep plenty in that part of the basin, swore those ancient pictures were older than Jesus himself, older than everything useful in the world except the Basques. They were not to be trusted.

Adams had never heard of a buffalo jump anywhere near the Gulch.

He led the gelding to his stall in the barn, the saddle loose but still on his back. Hobbs followed with the sorrel mare. Both horses had steam rising from their flanks. They smelled of sweat and mud. It was part crazy to ride out into the basin during the winter, but only part. A local jawboner hearing about Hobbs's trek would top the story with one of his own. That's the way it was out here: extremity as entertainment.

"It's not gonna be like it has been." Hobbs spoke from the realm of the sorrel mare's stall.

"What? What was that?" Adams's ears felt like they were wadded with cotton.

"N-not to be like it was."

"Okay, C.D. I think I got that." But he didn't. He realized he wasn't *getting* anything. He swiped at the roan's muscled shoulder with a soft brush, trying to organize the wariness that rippled through his legs and arms. C.D. was throwing down a fresh hand of cards. In fact, he seemed to be leading them into a whole new game, one where he was in charge of the rules. Hobbs in charge? Adams swallowed past his queasiness. He'd seen C.D. plunge into lopsided mental obsessions before. They always ended badly, especially for C.D. The man was never the last one standing.

Over the next week, Hobbs refitted the rear of the machine shed. He hung covered lights and tiered the orphaned tools and wired up a set of 120-volt outlets. He even got the old kerosene space heater working, though it looked to Adams like he neglected to take the heater into his room at night where it was needed. By the time he was finished, Hobbs had designed a workshop that was better than the one they'd had during their best days on the ranch.

"If you're trying to make me look bad," Adams joked, "it's working too damn well."

Hobbs asked if he needed permission.

"Permission for what?" Adams said. "You've never done a thing wrong when you've been fixing an item. Repairing. I doubt you're about to start."

Adams made himself assume that Hobbs wanted to fill his chilly February days by tinkering with the Trumpet Bell's idle machinery. But there was something about the new space—its surgical cleanliness, its stark organization—that unsettled him.

That Friday, he was in the barn trimming the horse's hooves when he heard the tenor whine of the grinder sing out from the cavern of the machine shed. He thought Hobbs might be shaping a new linchpin for the swather, a chore they'd discussed. After he stowed his tools and tossed the hoof scraps to the dogs, he yanked a gap in the shed's roll doors and paused to let his eyes adjust to the boxcar light. Beyond the guardian hulk of the tractors, he could see Hobbs in goggles, the smudge of his high-and-tight haircut dark on his skull. Hobbs making sparks.

Adams edged along a section of aluminum wall hung with busted shearing blades and a prideless collection of coyote pelts. He moved carefully until he came up on Hobbs's shoulder in a way only Rain, who was splayed on a folded tarp, noticed. He saw that Hobbs wasn't grinding a pin. Something else was gaining shape under his gloved hands. The air smelled of heat and ore and the stale breath of a slept-in room. Ghostly rings of smoke circled the burning lights. Adams wondered if Hobbs had been talking to himself. Not that it mattered. A man had a right to the music in his own head.

He stepped back from the bright arc of Hobbs's concentration and cleared his throat. He wasn't an intruder. He would make his presence known. Then he saw that Hobbs had set up a pair of vise grips near the end of the workbench. The grips were screwed tight into the plywood surface of the bench. Something large and intricate was clamped between them.

It looked like an open-ended badger trap, or a queer, slotted basket. Adams wasn't sure what it was. It might be the product of some therapeutic foolishness, though he had never known Hobbs to fool at a task when he wasn't in a hospital. The con-

traption shimmered like it was supposed to be pretty, which
it wasn't. He sidled closer, lassoed by the flare and smoke of
Hobbs's devotion to the grinder's wheel. The seams of Hobbs's
creation were smooth. They'd been expertly soldered. The interior surfaces were a starburst of aluminum scrap and chrome
and broken glass. For a noisy moment Adams was reminded
of Charlotte, how she had once wanted Hobbs settled on the
ranch in just this way, indulgently, pacifically, believing that
time and freedom and the tilted axis she called love could heal
him. She'd been wrong. There'd been no healing. Yet Hobbs
was here—when she wasn't—and he had his freedom.

At that moment Hobbs killed the grinder. Adams froze,
caught in the spotlight of his intrusion. But Hobbs didn't seem
at all surprised to see him. He pulled his goggles and gave
Adams a blue-eyed look of such predictable sanity that it was
as if the two of them had traded places. His coveralls glittered
with the sheen of hot metal filings. He said "Hello, Fremont,"
actually said the name, before he went to the far end of the
workbench and nipped something between the greasy fingers of
his doeskin gloves. He gave the thing to Adams. "Not done,"
he said, and then he waited.

Adams's first thought was of Christmas ornaments, for the
object in his hand was silvery and frail with just that kind of
cheap holiday profile. Then it came to him and his squinting
eyes all at once—the trim field jacket, the careless angle of the
shoulder-slung carbine, the purposeful O of the mouth. It was
Sergeant Jonas Devlin, Easy Company, 7th Marines. Etched, in-
cised, in posture. Adams swallowed an immediate liquid burning in his throat.

He gave Hobbs a pained, abandoned smile, a reaction that
was honest if it was not much else. He returned the figure, hoping to get rid of it before his hand got shaky. Sergeant Devlin in
effigy was defensible after all these years, maybe even desirable.
The sergeant had led their platoon of gunners in Korea. He had
made decisions that changed their lives. But Adams had only
to survey the structure between the vise grips—it looked more

cage-like to him now—to know that Hobbs wasn't finished
with his homemade rogue's gallery, not by a long shot.

He wasn't. Over the next few days he fashioned a navy
doctor from the hospital in Hungnam and a stunned portrait
of Pfc Ry Pilcher, which he crumpled underfoot. There was
also a prone figure of Adams himself, belly down with his machine gun. There was an arm-waving wildcatter who Hobbs
had drilled oil with in the 1960s. There were several sheep.
Adams didn't ask Hobbs why he was doing what he was
doing—he didn't dare—and he didn't fail to drop by the shed
every evening after the horses were settled. Not even when
Hobbs showed him, with a skittish fear of failure in his wrists,
a freshly snipped tin blank he somehow knew would come to
represent his lost sister Charlotte.

"I should have known," said Buren.

"It's not like he's calling me out, or showing how he might
go down the tubes again. He's just making these . . . things."
Adams felt compelled to contradict his brother, although he'd
been the one to phone and lay out the situation, if that's what
it was.

"*Life to me were misery . . .*"

"You do me no damn good with your quotes, thank you.
Not that you can do me much good anyhow. I just thought you
ought to know. I'm thinking of calling Charlotte."

He heard something that sounded like the stomp of a shoe
against Buren's refinished oak floor. "That, dear brother, would
be a mistake. C.D. should remember her as he remembers her,
which, from what you tell me, is a memory quite striking in its
passion. Perhaps he'll be content to create her likeness over and
over again, in the tradition of the spurned and betrayed. We
don't need to bring Charlotte into this."

"He's the one brought her in. It's like he's leading up to
saying—or doing—something that involves us all."

"He hasn't made a little statue of me, has he?"

Adams gave a sour chuckle. "No. Not yet. But you're not

free on this one, Buren. Don't pretend. You done things, too."
He couldn't believe how unshuttered the whole Hobbs thing
made him feel. He'd never thought of himself as a man who
judged other men's deeds or cast any lines of blame.

"Yes, I have." Adams listened for the catch of regret in his
brother's voice. He didn't hear it. "I'm right on this, nevertheless. You don't need to get in touch with Charlotte."

"What if she shows up?"

"How? Why? Do you think C.D. can just conjure her with
a bit of craft-fair handiwork? Nothing he does will make any
difference. Charlotte is finished with the men of the Trumpet
Bell. And the Trumpet Bell is finished with her. Her name is
off the deed, which is what you said you wanted. She can't get
back at you. But if you try to do something foolish that's meant
to absolve some of us—yourself, for instance—that's a different
story."

"I'm not absolving myself of anything. I feel a kind of hell
burn every day I see that man. I'm a big part of what ruined
him. But I want to know how to handle this. Am I just supposed to wait for another one of his medical episodes?"

"No." Buren's voice was soothing, certain. "You should
wait for an end. C.D. Hobbs has returned to our ranch to die,
I'm sure of it. There are many good reasons for him to do so,
not the least of which is he has no other home. You say he
looks as healthy as a grain-fed steer. Maybe so. But he's already
died twice over, as you no doubt vividly recall. He's a man of
peculiar symmetries."

"And I'm to stand by and let it happen."

"You don't whip the smolder into flames. That's my advice.
Let the poor, sick bastard direct his own encore."

Adams suffered a pang, a hot slicing across his body. He
wished Buren's words didn't sound so on the money. "I'd like
to. . . ."

"No, you wouldn't. You don't have what it takes to help
him. He doesn't need help—not from you, or any of us. Don't
lie to yourself about that. But if it makes you feel better," his

brother continued, "I'll pray to the best of my Episcopalian ability that your dear friend doesn't take you with him when he goes."

The next afternoon, during the kind of warm, still hour that bribed stockmen to hope for spring, Hobbs drove the Ford truck to the head of Ram Horn Creek. It was a change of routine, but Adams decided it didn't mean much. He didn't believe Buren was right about Hobbs wanting to die, so he preferred to imagine that most of Hobbs's motives, except for the ones he exercised in the machine shed, were still the equivalent of his own. This meant C.D. had probably gone to eyeball the ranch's dwindled ditches and aslant fences, the happenstance things a man does to seal himself to fallow land. He'd taken Adams's .30-06 in case he saw coyotes. And the dog, Rain.

Adams went to the shed. He couldn't kindle much desire to work on his unworkable ranch. He felt rooted in observation instead, drawn to watch over Hobbs's shrunken, flat-eyed cast of characters as they seemed to watch over him. He sat on the seat of the grinder—not too close, not too far away. The wind rose and fell over his solitude, and he listened to the eaves of the shed moan in imitation of far-flung human voices. Even when the Trumpet Bell had been failing all around him, the victim of low wool prices, high feed prices, busted cooperatives, foreign subsidies—the whole damn avalanche—Adams had made that failure into something he understood, something he could live with. He'd been raised to want the land, and he still had the land—ball and chain that it was. But his failures with Hobbs, large and small, were something he still didn't understand. How could somebody who loomed like drought, like a sky-blotting storm of locusts, keep settling into his life as the closest person he'd ever known?

Hobbs was unruffled when he returned to the shed, casual in the unsnapping of his caramel-colored coat. He seemed pleased to find Adams waiting in his place. In one sense, they had much to say to each other, men who had first learned the brutal weightlessness of words in the worthless foxholes of Chosin. Yet they hadn't spoken about those lost, forsaken days—not for decades. Adams knew all too well that relief wasn't a feeling either of them trusted.

"Your . . . project is going along good, C.D. Looks like you're making headway." Adams spoke from the powdered seat of the grinder. Rain crept to his spot on the tarpaulin.

But Hobbs misdirected Adams's words, the first sign things wouldn't go as they usually did. "The pasture out there needs a lot a work. Seeding. Fence. Healthy pronghorn, though. One buck tried to stand me off."

"Did you mention you'd be back in the fall with a license?"

"I did. Then I shot him where he stood."

Adams counted in his mind the number of times C.D. Hobbs had borne the authority he bore that moment beneath the black cowl of the shed. There weren't many. He didn't believe Hobbs had shot anything dead. But how did you ask a man about his lies or what he meant by trimming out people as paper dolls? Adams had spent some time studying the figure of Sergeant Devlin and the ever larger, glossier versions of Charlotte. He'd surveyed his own likeness with its unjammed machine gun. He'd stared at the oil-patch roughnecks with nail-scratched grins that Hobbs seemed to both love and hate. He'd stared at the ewes and the lambs and the dwarfish, weak-chinned doctors. They leaned against the walls of their small stage. They dangled from loops of scrounged-up twine; they gathered in unbalanced groups near the tin snips—every last one of them.

"F-fremont," Hobbs said, his voice raveling under the red kerchief he wore around his neck, "you seen it all."

And he had, hadn't he? The rock-ice hell of Hill 1281 at Chosin. The lowing calf love for Charlotte. That had been the worst of it—how his sister had tornadoed the feelings of a kind and vulnerable man. Then there was the infernal prank he and Buren had played to keep from being tainted by Hobbs's besotted craziness, a thing they claimed to have done to save the

Trumpet Bell. Yet the man kept coming back, no matter how soiled the memories. And now there was this: grooved, silver-scaled puppets without a puppeteer. Or a story to tell that might satisfy.

"You asked what I want to do," Hobbs continued. "It's a g-good question. I've thought it through day and night, without the doctors into it now. It's been fortysome years since you and me signed up in Cheyenne, all years of knowing and n-not knowing because sometimes my brain was mixed up and sometimes it weren't." He moved closer to his shantied crèche. He pointed at it happily, his head cocked to one side like a proud father above a crib. "You know all of them, that helps me. But you mightn't know this." He reached into the sections of soldered one-inch pipe that raftered the cage and freed a mis-shapen silhouette from its noose, slipped it to Adams.

Adams stared at the clotted figure that lay across his palm. He thought he understood the story here, and it was an ugly one. "Napalm," he croaked. "The captain called in the wrong coordinates for the ridge. He didn't mean to. . . ."

"Naw," Hobbs said, suddenly, horribly laughing. "This guy ain't from Lloyd Brewer's fried squad, though I remember that. The screaming. The smoke like off a barbecue. That was a mistake like only a man can make. N-no, this guy ain't Brewer. He ain't even from what you call our world. Our dimension. Somebody . . . different . . . was with us that night in Korea. I know it was a messed-up time, but I'm thinking you might have seen him on that hill and never told n-nobody. To be nice."

Adams felt a dangerous numbness spread through his chest, a numbness he knew from experience would reduce Hobbs to a putty he could store on a low, unimportant shelf. He remembered what Buren had said about encores. "We didn't see Chinese soon enough, that's what we didn't see."

"I recall the Chinese," Hobbs said calmly. "He was there, though. Or it. I h-hadn't quite got it all worked out. Boy or woman or what. I never saw no wings. Or a spaceship. The fellow I roomed with on the ward at Evanston said there had to be a sp-spaceship."

Adams sat ham-handed.

"I understand his purpose for the most part." Hobbs was solemn, searching Adams's dry, blinking eyes for an equal solemnity. "He'll come for me here again, like he did that time I was with Ch-Charlotte. He needs to finish his business. You're good that way, too. You know how to finish your business. You're off the irrigating, I finally figured that. But I can see the lambs coming. A new kind of lambs is coming, no matter what you say to me. We got important preparations to make. So I begun all this—"and he raised his arms like a conductor above the workbench and the tractors and the dog "—to get us ready."

II

Chosin Reservoir

Korean Peninsula

1950

THEY WERE TWO DAYS NORTH OF HUNGNAM, THE
weather thinning into a high altitude cold he recognized. Morning had arrived with a formation of gull-winged Corsairs that
passed over the rattling, coughing camp before turning to scan
the hills for North Koreans. The glass bulbs of the planes'
cockpits burned with the fire of the rising sun. It was a good
day to fly, Adams thought. The sky was clear and unclouded,
the color of quartz. It was a damn freezing day to move a war
into the mountains.

He was at the roadblock with his squad. Hobbs was there.
And Devlin. And everybody else except Fryberg who'd been
sent to the aid tent with his fever and pink, weepy eyes. They
were supposed to control the flow of refugees, which they'd
been trying to do since 0400. Nobody liked strong-arming
the farmers and their families, especially when it meant shaking down the old mama-sans and children. In Seoul, where he
and Hobbs had gotten their assignment three weeks earlier,
the boys and girls had smiled at the marines and begged for
gum and candy. Not here. Here the Communists hid among the
peasants, so every native who wanted to go behind U.S. lines
to Hungnam, where the Red Cross was passing out food and
blankets, had to be searched. And questioned.

Just now Sergeant Devlin had Ry Pilcher stirring through
the refugees' rice bags with his bayonet while Hobbs stood
guard over half a dozen men who'd been stripped naked by marines looking for grenades and guns. The squatting men were
lethargic from starvation and fear. The shadows among their
ribs were as blue as bruises. The rest of the refugees crowded
the barriers of the roadblock, anxious to get out of the path
of the converging armies. Adams could tell Hobbs hated his

assignment. His knees were locked tight above the buckled canvas of his leggings. His mouth was a thin, set line. There was no opportunity to play the good guy because he was out of chocolate. They all were. They had nothing to give the bony, whey-faced kids whose cheeks were aflame with exposure. All they could do was stand duty in their jackets and heavy boots while the greasy smell of their well-fed bodies mixed with the stink of pickled cabbage and shit that clung to the few rags of clothing the natives still had.

Adams blew into the palms of his hands. His skin was cracked and scaly, and one of his fingernails was split. He kept his fingers moving so they wouldn't get stiff in the cold. Devlin had put him in the machine-gun pit with Sutherland where he could afford an occasional glance at the peeled-back sky when he wasn't deciphering the road that lay before their position. He crouched to the left of the watchful Sutherland, ready to belt feed the .30 caliber light machine gun if necessary. He doubted it would be necessary. The N.K.s didn't come at a checkpoint head-on. It wasn't their style. If he concentrated, however, he could dull the disturbing sounds of the refugee interrogations the Republic of Korea soldiers were conducting behind the gun pit.

The ROKs were slapping the face of an older girl. He could hear the blows snap through the crisp air as the Koreans shouted, *Where is your brother? Where have you hidden his weapons? His comrades?* They asked the questions as if they were bandits asking for treasure, mechanically, with a cruel hint of languor. They didn't know whether the girl had a brother or not. They were looking for Reds in their own country, traitors, so they wanted to be thorough. It was a search that took time. Adams knew without checking that Hobbs still held his unblinking place, M1 at the ready, as the kneeling girl collapsed into a heap of noiseless sobs. Hobbs's six black-eyed, hollow-eyed farmers stood on their fleshless legs to dress themselves in the pitiless morning light. Pilcher continued to search the half-empty bags of rice.

Next to Adams, Sutherland tugged at the collar of his field

jacket as though some internal heat made the collar feel tight around his neck. His face, which was gashed by a thick set of eyebrows, remained impassive. Adams wondered if he and Sutherland shared the same acid thrum in their guts—from hunger, from the rough treatment they had witnessed. The long-necked manner in which Sutherland peered between the aiming stakes set before the gun suggested he wasn't itching for action, but with Sutherland you couldn't exactly ask. He was a twelve-year marine who'd been busted back to private for something excessive he'd done in Japan. He'd made it clear he didn't care for the new arrivals like Adams who'd been ass-tagged to Easy Company because it was short of men.

Devlin stuck his helmeted head over the sandbags and informed them that a patrol from Fox Company was coming into the lines. He reminded them of the password. Sutherland asked if the patrol had made any contact. Sergeant Devlin, a tireless collector of operational information, said that was what he'd come to find out. Neither of them mentioned the subdued herd of refugees corralled by mud and broken stone against their right flank.

A child began to wail. A child was always wailing unless the big guns were firing and all human complaint was erased in their recoil. The crying reminded Adams of orphaned lambs and how they filled acres of corrals and sheds with their inconsolable grief. The land the Americans were moving into offered other misplaced reminders of his Wyoming home: the biting promise of the valley wind, the black, wooded hillsides that recalled the elk country of the Sierra Madres. He shook his head to counter the thick pounding he felt in his sinuses. Only the U.S. Marine Corps could have shipped him from Bell Butte to California to Japan to a part of Korea so remote it began to feel familiar.

Like home, it was rough country. Steep and folded and bladed with granite ridges that looked no wider than a boot sole. The slender, exposed roads were barely more than cart paths. Adams knew it was bad ambush country just from looking at it. They all did. But to the salts like Sutherland and

Devlin who'd been on Tarawa and Iwo in the war before this one, the country was no worse than it had ever been. Enemy country was always bad. Evil. It was always sutured with bunkers filled with men who fought like hell. It didn't matter. They had no choice about it.

This was a truth hotter and more piercing than any bullet Adams could imagine. It throbbed beneath the skin of his body like a buried coal. He'd been in Korea less than a month, and it was time for him to learn to live without choice. There were certain deprivations that suited him—he knew this from his years on the ranch. But though he hated the stupid abiding military rules, he had come to hate his high-plains ignorance even more. He despised his lack of combat experience. He spit on his own greenhorn past. There was too much he didn't know, too much he had to grow into. The 7th Marine Regiment was headed toward the Yalu River on the Chinese border. The advance was removing his options with every step of every march. Things were likely to get rough. There could be only one goal: to become honed, all necessity. What remained of John Fremont Adams when it ended, however it ended, would be a distillation of man and pursuing soldier, a potent liquor brewed from what he believed and whatever he discovered in the high hills of Korea.

This was what he told himself.

He spotted the first of the men from Fox Company as they cleared a bend in the road that was half-blocked by a shattered ammunition trailer. The men trudged without chatter. They were unshaven, like everybody in camp, and footsore from climbing hills, and trousered in mud. Adams didn't see any stretcher bearers, but it was clear the patrol had stepped on somebody's wasp nest. Santo, the corpsman, was calling for a jeep. He had wounded men coming off the slopes. Adams counted the bandoleers of ammunition still worn by the B.A.R. men. One, two—there weren't many. Fox had left its share of metal jackets on the route then, plenty of them. Then came the prisoners, four smallish men in fur hats and green quilted uniforms—the first like those he'd seen. The prisoners moved with short, unlifted strides and carried their chins level, as if they were curious and temporary visitors.

"Christ and His Most Blessed Mother," said Sutherland.

Adams dropped to his haunches so his ear was at the level of the gunner's mouth. Despite Sutherland's silent bullying, Adams was supposed to anticipate his needs.

"Chinks," Sutherland said, "and not for the first time. MacArthur and his Tokyo generals better get ready to shit dry."

Adams looked again at the prisoners. He wondered how Sutherland could be so sure. The ROK soldiers had stopped their work; that might be a clue. The platoon lieutenant from Fox Company, a man whose name Adams didn't know, looked puckered up tight for a guy in safe from a midnight march, but lieutenants always looked that way. Was it the faces? Did somebody in Fox know the difference between Chinese talk and Korean? Gooks looked the same to him, as little as he'd seen them.

Devlin returned in a half crouch, his hands encased in a pair of homemade woolen socks. His smile was crooked and dangerous above his patchy reddish beard.

"Spoonhauer's coming to spring you for chow." The platoon sergeant's voice was whispery, almost girlish with its hints of secrets.

"You see that, Dev? You see what Fox fucking hooked on its line?" Sutherland was loud and guttural. Adams watched him squeeze the stock of the machine gun, as if he was personally offended by the sight of the prisoners.

Devlin hung a rictus smile in the air above Adams, his way of needling a buckass replacement private who knew no history. Then he replied to Sutherland. "I wasn't in Nanking with you Raiders, but I hear what you're saying. You're saying somebody's about to send us up the asshole of the whole Chinese army without a warning. God damn Tokyo command." Devlin shook his helmeted head so hard his shouldered carbine began to sway. "Wish I could send you to H.Q. to straighten out those map-reading bastards, Suds, I really do. Best I can do is report that the captain's sending out Third Platoon tonight. We'll be attached. Tell me who you want."

Sutherland hawked something upward into his mouth, then wall-eyed Adams while he seemed to savor the slickness that floated on his tongue. "We got baby shit."

"Sure," said Devlin, "but I'm asking."

"I'll take this one. He's quiet." Sutherland stared out over the black angles of his gun. "Not the whiner, though, and not the other cowboy, he won't stick in a hard fight. Maybe the spic if I have to."

"I'll talk to the lieutenant."

"We got one of those now?"

"Yeah. Reservist. From Vir-gin-i-a." Devlin spoke the state's name as if were a part of France.

Sutherland spat a white gob onto the straw mat Adams had unrolled in the bottom of the gun pit to pad his knees. "Sweet Mother of God."

"May She be with us on this night," Devlin crooned. Then he was gone, swifter and more affable than he had a right to be.

Sutherland jammed his hands into his pockets and began to curse in his name-filled Catholic way. His square chin jabbed outward with every word. He fiddled with the gun sights, then barked at Adams for a cigarette, which Adams had to fork over. Adams wanted to ask Sutherland what he knew about the Chinese. They'd trained the North Koreans, the Chinese had, and the N.K.s hadn't been hard to handle since Pusan. That's what Pilcher and Fryberg said. But maybe the Chinks had maneuvers they hadn't shared with the N.K.s. Devlin and the other veterans acted like that was true for the marines, like they believed the corps had been holding itself back, was still doing so, waiting for the professional sons-a-bitches to take the field. The Chinese had done nothing but wage war for thirty years. They hadn't been lying in their hammocks on Okinawa or shucking good soldiers from their full-strength regiments. They hadn't been playing politics. If the Chinese got into things, the Americans were going to have their hands full.

Adams drew in the harsh smell of Sutherland's cigarette until his mouth began to water. He decided to smoke one himself. He was about to go on his first night patrol. He vowed he wouldn't ask questions or appear too eager about anything. He'd just be ready to do the job, whatever Devlin or Sutherland said the job was. There wasn't much a soldier had to understand about an enemy before his first fight. He'd heard plenty of guys say that. A long, hard day in Korea appeared simpler if you thought about it that way, or an hour.

Spoonhauer's squad arrived right on time. There was no talk in the pit until the new gunner and assistant settled in. Hobbs and Pilcher backed off the refugee line where shawls and straw hats flapped like broken bird wings in the breeze. They set up on the machine gun's flanks until Devlin waved them all in. The sergeant didn't mention the upcoming patrol so Adams stayed shut about it. C.D. was talkative as he often was after a tense stretch of duty. He tended to behave like a spigot, on and off and on. Sometimes he wanted to talk about baseball, a passion he'd learned to imitate at Camp Pendleton. Sometimes he wanted to talk about food or some strange Korean thing he'd seen. Today it was letters.

"I just got a thing I want you to tell Charlotte. One thing, not a whole page worth. And hello to Old Etchepare from me. He'd be amazed by this country, don't you think, how sorry it is for livestock except for the water. It can't be a bit like France where he fought in that trench war. And will you say something about those Mongol ponies we seen? I bet those ponies would handle a winter logging camp in the Madres just fine, they got the build for it. Sergeant said to get breakfast and grab sack time until 1200. Are you worn out because I'm not. I thought I'd be tired. I should be tired. You're going to write home today, right? Take a minute?"

Adams flattened his red hands until they were like trowel blades, then made an exaggerated attempt to peer under the brim of Hobbs's helmet. Hobbs hadn't changed much physically during their slogging weeks in the corps. He hadn't shaved for several days, but it made less of a difference with him since he grew no hair on his face to speak of, even though he was nineteen. There were kids in the company who were younger than Hobbs, younger than both of them. None of them had the unblended look of Hobbs.

"There's not much to say, C.D. We can't talk about chasing Commies in letters. It gets censored."

"We could tell something about Japan to Buren except he's at the college in Laramie. And greetings to your ma and father."

"Do it yourself," he said, wanting to occupy himself with nothing but steaming hot coffee. "You know how to write."

Hobbs pulled up at the rear bumper of an officer's jeep, halting his progress toward the mess tent. "She don't give a rat's shit where I am, what I do," he said, meaning his feckless mother who was supposedly shacked up with a government trapper near Kremmling, Colorado. Adams hadn't meant to bring Hobbs's mother into it. He'd been thinking of his own family, who wrote often to them both, or claimed to. They hadn't received much mail since California. They'd been moving too fast.

"Come on," he said to Hobbs. He walked his friend forward with such definition the grenades in their webbed belts beat hard against their hips. There was a long line of latecomers at the mess tent. It would do him and Hobbs both good if they decided they were hungry. "I hope you got a plan if I get hurt, though, or when I get that influenza Fryberg's been breathing all over. I hope you got a extra postman in reserve."

"You don't need to talk that way, Fremont." Hobbs kept pace, but he sounded genuinely gaffed under his helmet and coat.

"Why not? You think words like that ought to be secret? We're machine gunners, and Sergeant says the whole damn Chinese army is waiting for us up this road. It don't matter what we say in talk." Adams felt the dismissal of his body, and his future, flood his veins right then and there, cleansing him of fatigue and anxiety all at once. He welcomed any opportunity to make superstitions public, especially his own. "Talk don't make anybody less safe."

Hobbs stopped again, and Adams braked his own heels. Soldiers passed them, some sauntering, others dragging their legs beneath their spines like weary cattle. All bore the red-rimmed gaze of sleeplessness and want. Hobbs's face, what Adams could see of it, went still and unflushed. He said, "I know you'll be all right."

As a further sign of benediction, the air around them suddenly tore itself in half as howitzers from the 11th Marines began to register on distant targets they couldn't see. There were more Corsairs in the air as well, trailing dirty smoke.

"Hell on you, C.D., if you know so much. Let's get breakfast while there's something left to get." Adams gave Hobbs what was meant to be a friendly punch on the arm, but he hated how he was pretending to be cheerful. What difference did it make? Hobbs was on a slide. Most of the new guys were, feeling down sometimes and then up, feeling whipped side to side, careening, as their abilities began to fall short of what was demanded of them. His own confidence tended to slip from moment to moment, and they hadn't even done any fighting yet. Their relentless drill instructors had warned them about this danger, had tried to prepare them for it during the hurried time they had to fill the depleted marine ranks. But how did you train men for constant onslaught, inside their heads and out?

Adams knew this was why Hobbs might be left off the night patrol. Sutherland didn't think C.D. and Begnini, who he called a whiner, had developed the right stomachs for the job. Adams didn't know exactly why Sutherland thought that. Hobbs hauled gear as well as any of them, and he never complained about a single thing. But Sutherland had decided Hobbs was weak. Adams allowed himself a controlled moment of worry. He didn't think C.D. was weak, that wasn't the word he would use, but he wondered if the exclusion would be a problem. Hobbs liked it when the two of them stayed together,

and maybe he liked it that way, too, if he was honest about it.
They hadn't been separated very often. But the sergeants had
say on patrols. He and Hobbs hadn't been given a choice.

Adams shoved through the flaps of the squad tent into the wavy
green light produced by the kerosene stove. The air was thick
with a stale, outpost warmth. He stripped off his field jacket
and the gloves he was allowed to wear when he was not manning the gun. Some of the men were out mailing letters. Others
were seeing a corpsman about blisters or bartering for beer and
cigarettes or taking a rare crap. The rest were near their cots,
moving quietly like animals in their stalls.

Hobbs, it seemed, had been coaxed into telling some of
his stories. Miguel Rocque, who was from right in the city of
Houston, Texas, liked Hobbs's stories, and he often asked for
one while the squad was cleaning its weapons. Adams made
his way down a narrow aisle, then laid his coat on his cot. He
ducked out of his heavy helmet. The drugstore reek of Rocque's
hair tonic was stronger than usual, and it made a poor mix
of smells with the kerosene from the stove. Ry Pilcher seemed
to be swabbing the hair tonic directly onto the grooved metal
of his disassembled M1. That was news. Pilcher was taking
Sergeant Spoonhaur's advice. Spoonhauer, who'd fought at the
Bulge against the Germans, claimed hair tonic was better than
standard-issue gun oil if you wanted to keep a gun firing in
the cold.

"Butch Cassidy had his Hole-in-the-Wall boys, see. And they
started robbing Union Pacific trains in the desert. . . ."

It sometimes took Adams a moment to recognize C.D.
Hobbs's entertainer voice when he heard it. C.D. had been a
talker back home, but not the sort anybody really listened to.
Since the marine-recruit depot in San Diego, however, there'd
been a fullness to Hobbs's public speech, an almost athletic
confidence. His Wyoming stories featured a graceful patience
that Adams realized Hobbs must have been hoarding for years.
This patience led Hobbs to select details for his stories as carefully as another man might select a string of packhorses. He

brought to life the fables and jokes of all the ranch hands he had ever known. It was a good trick, Adams thought. It gave Hobbs a piece of a bigger reputation and made him appear natural at living outdoors among men.

"One-eared Ike Dart was a colored slave who become a good cowboy before he started stealing folks' cattle. He lost his ear to a Ute woman with a axe, if you can believe that. They say she did it for love. . . ."

Hobbs, Adams thought, was nothing *but* natural. And gullible. He knelt to unclasp the top of his field pack. There were two photographs in a plastic sleeve near the top of the pack. One was a picture of his dun horse, Jackson, who was only three years old and still needed a firm hand. The other was a picture of his family taken at an ice-cream social in Savery. His father and Buren were both in ties and shirtsleeves. His mother and Charlotte wore matching summer dresses. Would the people in that photograph still recognize him, he wondered. Had he become as different as he needed to be?

He slipped the photos inside his field jacket, then paused to see if Hobbs would tell the one about Miss Minni, the Rawlins brothel keeper, and her trick poodle dog. That story was one of Hobbs's favorites. It didn't seemed to matter to anybody that Hobbs had never set foot in Miss Minni's railroad hotel or never laid eyes on the poodle or Miss Minni's infamous .44 caliber pistol. Hobbs's first real try at whoring had come in Japan, and the attempt had resulted in a story Hobbs wasn't likely to tell on this afternoon.

Ry Pilcher, a grocer's son from Alabama, interrupted Hobbs. "That is a pure damn lie," he snorted, trying not to laugh through his nose. "You've primed us with whoppers before, cowboy, but I ain't listening to this one. It's as bad as the bull you shoveled about that damn outlaw in his pickle barrel."

"Shut up," Rocque said. He'd wiped the hair tonic from his hands and was trying to roll a fresh cigarette. "I want to hear what he says. Leave him alone."

Pilcher coughed until his eyes were shiny. "The cowboy is pulling your sweet Texas leg, Rocque, but if that's the way you want it, be my guest. I bet Big Adams over there can set you straight." Pilcher waggled a finger in Adams's direction. "Give it to them, A-man. Tell us you didn't really find no famous gunman salted down like one of my daddy's hams."

But they had, sort of. It depended on how you told the story. He and Hobbs and little Charlotte had driven to Rawlins that past spring to buy supplies at the mercantile. They'd gone to Molander's to gawk at the new Chrysler sedan that was fresh off the train. They'd bribed Charlotte with two cherry Cokes to sit on the sidewalk while they went into Addington's to shoot some pool. They were on their way to the no-name Mexican restaurant that served cheap food to sheepherders and ranch hands when Charlotte spotted a crowd gathered at the excavation site for Hested's new store. She was off like a shot, the brat. Before Adams could catch her, she'd wormed through the crowd and slid down a muddy plank into the half-dug foundation. Two sweating excavators had just wrestled an ancient whiskey barrel from where it had been buried near an old foundation. The workers knew the barrel wasn't sloshing with whiskey, so they claw-hammered it open, and the first thing that got to them was the stink. The second thing that got to them was the sight of a hand and arm bobbing in a moss-colored broth of formaldehyde and brine. Charlotte snuck close enough to see the show. Then she vomited all over her starched pinafore and Sunday shoes.

"Big Nose George," Adams said. "They really did bury him that way. Nothing Christian about it. He got lynched in the old days for killing two deputies, then stuffed into a barrel. It was what he deserved."

"And your governor skinned him out and made himself up a pair of shoes," Rocque crowed. "Don't forget that part. I never heard anything so *loco*."

Adams grinned. "The governor did tan some of George's hide. The rest went into that barrel. After sixty years, it weren't a pretty sight."

Adams tried to catch Hobbs's eye as he finished his version of the tale, but Hobbs kept his head down while he reassembled his gleaming rifle. Hobbs had really helped him out that day. Adams had been so angry at Charlotte, so embarrassed, that he'd wanted to slap her, but Hobbs kept the lid on, using his own shirttail to wipe the vomit from Charlotte's soiled pinafore. Hobbs had assured Adams's little sister that it wasn't chicken to puke when you saw a dead man. By the time they'd driven the fifty dusty miles back to the Trumpet Bell, Charlotte was as sassy as she'd ever been—if a little ripe smelling. She and Hobbs filled the truck cab with groans and wails and other mummy sounds they attributed to an unburied, revenge-seeking Big Nose George.

A few weeks later, as high-school graduation drew close and the newspapers ran worrisome columns about collaboration between the Russians and the Chinese, an army recruiter arrived hat in hand at the grange hall in Baggs. Maybe it came from missing the big war against the Germans and the Japs, maybe it came from wanting to get out into the world they'd heard about from Etchepare and Uncle Gene—but he and Hobbs soon found themselves on a train to Cheyenne where they volunteered to be marines. To Adams, the enlistment was like stringing one more bead onto a slender string, year after year, event after event, Hobbs never holding him back, Adams never obstructing Hobbs. Now they were in a place called Sudong on Sergeant Jonas Devlin's smeared, inaccurate map, and they were stringing on more beads, faster. Times were changing. They were changing. Adams was glad C.D. was liked by the other men, that he had an easy capacity for friends. He, himself, didn't feel the same need for company, though he liked how it happened among the others—the impulse, the crafted talk and laughter. He believed it could only be good for him to step into his days with those sounds in his head for as long as they might last.

Devlin wasn't leading the patrol, but he might as well have been. The new lieutenant from Virginia was smart enough to let his sergeants run the squads. There were squads from mortars and squads from machine guns, in addition to Third Platoon's riflemen and Hebert, the regular corpsman. Even with attachments, the patrol was under strength. That wasn't supposed to be a problem since their job wasn't to defeat the enemy but to find out where he'd laid his lines.

"Let me tell *you* bastards what the *Chink* bastards been telling the intelligence pinkies which you are not supposed to know." Devlin wasn't conspiratorial now. He was still in the bulk of his buttoned jacket and thick flannel shirts, poised and watchful, like a hawk in a barren tree. It wasn't how Adams had imagined his sergeant whom he thought of as mischievous and catlike in attitude even when his business was serious. The skin of Devlin's face was pasty under its smears of burned cork, and Adams could see newly deepened hollows under his eyes. There was a rumor that the sergeant had contracted the influenza but would in no damn way go off the patrol because he didn't think much of the other noncoms except for Sutherland who'd lost his stripes. Adams didn't believe the rumor. Devlin didn't look sick to him.

"The bastards are bragging to the running dog capitalist soldiers of the United States of America. They say they've got a whole division up there." Devlin gestured in the direction of their jump-off point. "They claim there are ten divisions south of the Yalu where we're going for our riverside picnic with the 8th Army. They've given names, numbers, armament—every little thing but current addresses—because they invite war with the marine butchers and their imperialist generals. Tokyo says this is Commie prop-o-ganda bullshit, Chinese got nobody down here but a few hundred volunteers with the N.K. If you want me or the lieutenant to tell you what this really means, we can do it right now."

Adams turned his head until he could see Sutherland squatting next to the light machine gun. He'd been assigned to carry ammunition for Sutherland. The older man was smoking and working the thongs that held his dog tags between a tight thumb and finger. His brown, close-set eyes were no more than slots. He seemed comforted by every syllable of bad news Devlin uttered.

Devlin went on. "We're going out quiet, no helmets, and keep your canteens and bayonets secure. You're supposed to have an extra day's rations so you better have them. Password is 'Deep Purple,' don't forget it. I'll say this. This is the Chinks' country, and they're good at what they do. We'll have to be better. Checkpoint will pass us through in ten minutes, so do your pissing and coughing now."

Adams watched as the lieutenant laid out the order of march. A man on point would be followed by a rifle squad that included the lieutenant and his radioman. A mortar section would go next, then Sutherland's gun crew, more riflemen, the second section of mortars, etc. Rocque would be Sutherland's assistant. Adams and a kid named Greenbaugh were to lug a box of .30 caliber belts between them. Pilcher was back with Spoonhauer and the second machine gun.

Adams studied the white oval of the rising moon. It looked like a storm lantern hung just out of reach. The wind that rushed past his face bore the familiar, metallic taste of snow on its edge. He knew the wind would muffle their advance just as it obscured any movement by the Chinese or North Koreans. This wasn't hunting, Adams told himself. When a man went hunting, he most often went onto land that was familiar and in conditions that were in his favor. This was blindness. And a kind of provocation. He knew he'd appreciate his bulky dress as the temperature fell, and he knew his well-worn boots wouldn't give him any trouble. But he would be slower· than usual with the ammunition to carry. This made him uneasy. Devlin had made it clear that action—especially action at night—sometimes spooked new guys, and he didn't want to be the one who spooked.

The men drew themselves into formation. Adams saw Sutherland wave to him, and he moved closer to the gunner with Greenbaugh by his side. Sutherland had a wool cap and a felt-lined hat pulled tight over his wide forehead. He told them to get ready to hoist their load. "I want to say something about the fucking Chinks that maybe Dev don't feel the need to say." The guttural voice smelled bitterly of cigarettes. "I want to say they ain't as cocky or desperate as the N.K.s. They'll wait us out. They got discipline, and they don't go stupid. But they like their bottleneck ambush coming from high ground just like the god damn Sioux did, so they'll take their chance if they fucking get it which is likely in this hellhole terrain. You don't want to get caught by them. You don't want to be their prisoner." His pinpoint eyes telescoped to the guarded barrier of a memory. When the eyes returned to their waiting faces, they reflected a wet, prismed anger. "Best advice you'll ever get."

They got the signal and passed through the line manned by Dog Company. They didn't receive the usual taunts from their fellow marines, and they knew this was because of the crush of refugees and the unruly flight of the Republic of Korea army, which seemed to be dissolving in front of them. It wasn't long before they could barely hear the noises of the camp, the tight fart of the diesel engines, the orchestra of aluminum and steel that crashed above the more easily dispersed murmurs of men. Adams and Greenbaugh shifted hands on the handles of the ammunition box. Its weight was awkward and cut off the circulation of their fingers even when they wore gloves. While they were on the road they found it easier to walk side by side, which they wouldn't be able to do on paths in the hills.

As the patrol snaked forward, Adams heard movement, panicked and sudden, from the roadside ditches. He was prepared for this. There were refugees to consider. And ROK deserters. They were supposed to be careful about firing at anything along a road. The drainages around Sudong were also full of small Korean deer that were high-hocked and quick. "There's another one," Greenbaugh whispered, nodding toward the tangled brush. Greenbaugh was from near Chicago, but every fall he took his deer meat from the forests of Wisconsin. He'd been watching the roads and ditches for several days. "They're being pushed out of their cover," he said. "Whatever's in those mountains has got them on the run."

He hadn't even said good-bye to Hobbs. C.D. was gearing up for the patrol when Devlin came into the squad tent and called his name. Hobbs followed the sergeant with his rifle and helmet in hand, but not his pack. He carried his shoulders loose in their sockets as though he expected to return. He hadn't. Devlin had walked him straight to the command post to meet with the captain.

He thought of Hobbs as they crossed the small creeks that were silvered with ice, as they toiled through underbrush at the base of the black, treed slopes that towered over them. Hobbs would probably compare the patrol to night duty with the sheep herd. With sheep, you sometimes had to stay out until dawn tracking a lion or coyote. You sometimes had to scout for a lost band of ewes and lambs in the darkness as carefully as you'd scout an enemy. Except this wasn't the same as herding sheep. It couldn't be. You didn't have your dogs, for one thing. What you had instead was the huffing and banging of thirty men trying to maintain a silence that couldn't be maintained. And you weren't going to get shot at when you were with sheep. Not normally. The biggest danger in those mountains was lightning.

Adams wondered if Hobbs was thinking of him. He'd seen men marking time in camp after they'd been taken off assignment. They looked uncomfortable, shrunken, as if they'd been drenched in the wrong kind of rain. How would C.D. handle it? Would he sleep off his disappointment or twist himself into a double barb of energy? Adams wished he'd been able to say a few words to Hobbs, to explain himself. Because now, as the hours passed and the wind began to needle his skin with invisible sleet, he felt himself begin to drift. Maybe it was the fatigue. Maybe it was the endless valley they were in, the way the patrol's path wound into a complete and foreign darkness, but Adams found he couldn't conjure up a clear image of C.D.'s face. Only the weather remained real to him. And the quiver of his exhausted muscles. The slow stumble of Greenbaugh's feet was also very real. Nothing else mattered for the moment. What else could matter? C.D. Hobbs, whoever he was, was not part of this struggling body. C.D. Hobbs had been left far, far behind.

A few hours before dawn they struck a trail that ran north. Somebody had recently used the trail, that was obvious, so they waited while the lieutenant sent out scouts. The place was a wallow of long-bladed grass and stagnant water that would have been brown with tannins if they could have seen it. Rocks were notched like teeth along the length of a mucky creek bed. The lieutenant quickly decided he wanted them on better ground. They would climb a small hill to the west, then cross a narrow, unprotected saddle to a longer ridge that led south. The lieutenant was afraid they had put themselves behind more enemy than they could handle. He was fresh from Virginia, but he still had that feeling. Adams would later be told that the scouts had heard Chinese pickets talking to one another as they withdrew up the northern trail. The scouts had gotten close enough to smell garlic on the pickets' breath.

Climbing the hill was awkward business because of the heavy ammunition box and the eroded soil that gave way under their feet. Adams and Greenbaugh scrambled as well as they could, both of them working their thighs in short, paired strokes like pistons. Adams slid onto his face more than once. The earth that worked its way into his mouth tasted of frozen, unliving rock before he spit it out.

Sergeant Devlin knew what to look for on the hilltop, and he found it—a shallow, elongated pit already scraped out for a gun. The pit afforded a clear field of fire across the saddle toward the southern ridge. Devlin also found some enemy soldiers, a small number of them, abandoning the crest as he and a team of riflemen elbowed themselves over the top. A marine with a big .50 caliber Browning Automatic Rifle began to fire at the departing soldiers before Devlin could stop him. The lone cough of the B.A.R. made Adams's pulse double. "Nothing but scouts," Devlin hissed. "They wanted us to see them. Get the gun up. We need to secure this spot because what those S.O.B.s will do is try to keep us off that next hill, which is our way home." And he pointed into the jabbing wind toward a raised brow of stone they couldn't even see.

Adams couldn't remember taking cover behind a comb of brush with Greenbaugh. He felt his sweat go clammy against his skin, but he did not identify its chill as a discomfort. It was just there like the light of the moon was there, blue and withdrawn. The enemy did return to probe their position. Sutherland was ordered not to fire the machine gun until necessary because they didn't want the enemy to mark it. Uneven rifle fire crack led around the perimeter, then a precious illumination round from one of their own mortars lit the sky, and they could see men bellying across the saddle under the false, stagy light, all of them in green quilted coats. Chinese, not Korean.

The rifle fire from the marines rose in pitch. Adams saw men trying to ascend the steep slope below him and below Greenbaugh. The sight choked him with adrenaline. Greenbaugh rolled a grenade downhill, then another. He hurried the first one, but the second one shattered the incline with light. Adams fired his rifle several times in that direction, but his fire went unanswered. He reloaded, striving for something like efficiency even as he paused to vomit from a stomach that held no food.

Soon there was shouting and gunfire from all points; it made orientation nearly impossible. Adams swore to himself, over and over, that he wouldn't spook, and he watched for the floating shadow that was Devlin. He watched Sutherland, who seemed to operate at a deliberate, balletic pace, keeping Rocque calm as Rocque fed the icy belts of brass cartridges into the chittering gun that they'd begun to fire. Devlin came to them, flick-eyed and kneeling, his gaze thick with some kind of internal purpose but fixed directly on their faces. He told Adams and Greenbaugh to sling whatever ammunition they could carry onto their shoulders. He would lead them forward, shortly. All the way across that damn saddle.

Adams tried to look at Greenbaugh, tried to ask Greenbaugh if he was all right. Greenbaugh's breath was steaming so hard and fast from his lungs it seemed as if he must be hurt. But Greenbaugh wasn't hurt. The two of them peered again over the drop-off to their left. It was like peering into a quarry filled with undisturbed water. Then Devlin waved them out.

He saw some of them get hit. A rifleman buckled to his knees in front of him. And he high-stepped over another splayed shape as he ran parallel to the hot red stitchery of the tracers from Spoonhauer's machine gun. There was shouting, some of it from pain, some from haste and fear. The marine mortars were pummeling the high ground now, and it was their luck the Chinese had no mortars. Sutherland and Rocque got their gun two-thirds of the way across a narrow bridge of land that looked as gray as cement under their racing feet before Rocque was hit. Bullets took the meat from his right shoulder. Sutherland pumped his arm to draw Adams forward, and he was there, ready to set the bipod under the gun while they hunkered in a shallow depression made by their own mortar shell. The corpsman found Rocque lying conscious in his geometry of bandoleers. He could use his legs. Greenbaugh was on his stomach to Adams's left. The hood of his jacket had fallen away from his blackened face, which was panting but expressionless, wiped clean by exertion. Adams wondered if he looked that way. He fought the need to make noise as he exhaled. The lieutenant came up with his radioman. The lieutenant asked Sutherland if he could make it to the base of the hill. There was apparently some trouble with the other machine gun.

No, he told Sutherland, he hadn't seen Devlin. They were taking fire on the right and needed to get over the ridge before they were pinned down. Sutherland should consider himself in charge of the gunners because if the mortars could quiet the single Chinese gun on the heights, the rest would be up to him.

The Chinese machine gun fanned green tracers from left to right and back again. Adams could no longer separate the low pitch of the Chinese burp guns from other rifle fire. Men crawled past him. A concussion grenade from up top showered him with grit and a wetness he felt but couldn't see. When more marines stood to rush over him, Sutherland lifted Adams by his webbed belt and moved the black cave of his mouth with urgency. It was time to go. He was deaf from the grenade, and he hadn't even known it.

They took the heights and the tentlike ridge that stretched toward their camp. A B.A.R. man shut down the Chinese machine gun with flanking fire and grenades, and he got a chest wound for his trouble. They had a total of eight wounded, two of them bad enough to need carrying. They counted seven dead Chinese left on the field. And one of their own was missing. It was Devlin.

Sutherland demanded they stay and search. The corps did not leave men behind, ever. He screamed this aloud, the code everybody swore by, and two noncoms who'd known him and known Devlin for a long time held him back and kept him off the brand-new lieutenant. The lieutenant asked Spoonhauer when he'd last seen Devlin, and the gunner, whose jacket and pants had been shredded by shrapnel along one side of his body, couldn't say. The lieutenant, who was a lawyer back in Virginia and a good one, sent volunteer scouts back along the saddle, but he told Sutherland a longer search was too dangerous. They had wounded to get home. The Chinese might regroup and come back in force. He ordered Sutherland to stay with his squad and prepare to move on. Sutherland complied with a rigidity of voice and bone that frightened Adams. It was the only time all night he felt that way: overwhelmed by the actions of another man.

Adams drew stretcher duty. He and a private named Dominick and two others tried to carry the wounded B.A.R. man. The B.A.R. man thrashed with pain and threw himself from the stretcher made of rifles and ponchos. They had to strap him down while he fought them, and a collapsed lung caused his breath come in long, sucking rattles that were terrible to hear. At one point, they dropped the B.A.R. man on a slippery decline, and he screamed through the blood in his mouth until Hebert gave him as much morphine as he could take. He died in agony and froth less than a mile from camp as he prayed into their bent, striving faces with verses they couldn't understand. His desperate attempt to communicate left Adams's own mouth shrunken and dry. Hebert closed the bulged eyes and tagged the body, and they shrouded him, the B.A.R. man, and the other stretcher-borne man who had died on the ridge soon after the fight, in their own ponchos, which were brittle with cold.

At the end of the final mile, Adams watched Sutherland make his way through the Dog Company lines with their machine gun across his back like a yoke. The dawn air was light enough to reveal the gun's seared and smoky vents and Sutherland's ferocious, bitten weariness. Adams could see also the blackish blood of the dead B.A.R. man on the gloves of his own hands. The blood had soaked him to the wrists. He worked in his seized, upended mind to halt the impending belief that the blood somehow belonged to Devlin.

Hobbs was waiting near the squad tent, but not in it. His eyes and hands leaped when he saw Adams, though he said nothing that might embarrass Adams or embarrass them both. Pilcher took a long, flat look at Hobbs, then told him about Devlin, who was Missing In Action, and about Rocque, and about the two men from Third Platoon who had been killed. Pilcher wanted to talk about all of it, he wanted to get it out, but he was too steamrollered to make much sense. Some of the other men lay down on their cots instead of walking across the camp to eat or get hot coffee. Adams, too, wanted to lie down and squeeze his eyes shut. He wanted to get off his aching feet. But the blind confinement of the tent made the skin of his face feel like melting wax, so he came back out into the morning where the camp was a bright game board of vehicles and stacked supplies and men who looked smaller than they should.

He asked Hobbs for a cigarette. Hobbs gave him one and

pulled a lighter from his dungarees, and they both began to smoke with their eyes shelved against the morning glare. Adams's hands continued to tremble. He didn't care if Hobbs saw his hands. He asked Hobbs about his visit with the captain. Hobbs shied to one side as if he didn't want to talk about that business, not first, but he went on with it when he sensed how Adams needed him to lay out a series of events that could be readily understood. The captain was fine, he said. He was just looking for some help.

Adams smoked his cigarette to the pinch of his fingernails before he stripped the damp butt and threw its pieces to the ground. His lips were so split and sore he could taste his own juices. "Captain could use you. He'd be lucky to have you running wire or being on the radios. You could go for Pfc over there." He talked in a neutral tone, which took great effort. He could taste the tears that flowed behind his teeth.

Hobbs shook his head. "I told him I wouldn't leave Weapons Platoon unless he ordered me to. Told him I appreciated the offer, that I was flat scared of his appreciation. He asked why I didn't want to come over, and I told him I only knew how to do things with the gunners, and he asked me why I didn't want to learn more, and I said I wanted to be a better marine at my assigned job first. He liked that."

"You could have asked him to put you on motor transport." Adams looked at his fat, aching fingers. They had almost stopped shaking. He had thrown his gloves away to be burned. "You could be king mechanic of the motor pool."

"So could you, and you're here," Hobbs said. His upper body went rigid with an emotion Adams didn't recognize. He sipped at the cold morning air with gray lips. "I just said I'd stay with weapons if Sergeant Devlin and the lieutenant would have me. It's the place I was put."

"We don't have Devlin now. We lost him." Adams tried to smooth the screech out of his voice.

Hobbs removed his helmet. He held it in front of him like a dark, empty basket. The damp pupils of his eyes were strangely blank and still. "I'm not clear on that yet, why it had to happen," he said. "But I knew you'd be all right, Fremont. I knew it all along. I did. Just like I know I wouldn't have been."

Devlin was found the next night by a team at a listening post. He had crawled within range of the post, then rolled himself onto an open stretch of road until the men assigned to the post got permission to investigate. He had taken one bullet in the calf, which left his leg swollen and oozing, and one through the jaw, which caped his field jacket with blood. He had come for miles somehow, bleeding and emptied by shock. He didn't last another night.

Sutherland found a Chinese canteen on Devlin's belt and Chinese uniform insignia, which had been cut free with a knife, in his pockets. Sutherland stayed as close to Devlin as the surgeons would allow, he even spoke a few words with the sergeant, but he didn't share the details with a single soul. He became like an aimed spear around the lieutenant and everybody else. The other noncoms gathered with mugs of weak coffee to talk about Devlin and what he'd done and how he deserved to survive this puny-ass war after what he'd been through with the Japanese in the last. They told themselves that he had burrowed like a wolf during the day to avoid capture. Somebody had seen the shell of mud on his uniform that proved it.

Devlin's loss was a bad one, though nobody said it was unexpected. There was no use talking about it for long—Devlin wouldn't have stood for the nattering, and it was the way of the veterans to bury a man when he was buried. But the gunners took the news hard. They tried all manner of things to barricade themselves with luck. Pilcher visited the chaplain. Spoonhauer shuffled and reshuffled his red-backed deck of cards. Adams replayed versions of the patrol in his head that ended with triumph and relief. Even Sutherland was seen worrying the black beads of a rosary. Rumor had it that the rosary had belonged to Devlin.

Hobbs tried to relax the men in the gunner's platoon by telling a few choice stories, but all his efforts seemed to go wrong. Because Sergeant Devlin had so obviously tried to have Hobbs transferred to another unit, most of the men thought it was out of line for Hobbs to participate in their grief. When Hobbs talked about the Green River mountain man who had once shot a bear for breakfast, Pilcher stopped him. Pilcher thought the story was disrespectful. When Hobbs worked up a good head of steam with a set of adventures that featured the cattle detective Nate Champion, he had to ease off as it became clear his restless audience would not tolerate the final episode that described Nate's death during a fiery ambush. Nobody except Rocque wanted to hear Hobbs's anxious, distracting rambles, and Rocque was soon shipped back to Hungnam because of his shoulder wound. Only the navy corpsmen, who labored in the now crowded aid tents, could stand to be around C.D. Hobbs. They didn't care if he was an outcast or a nutcase or a shirker. They didn't care what he said, or how he said it, as long as he was willing to handle bedpans and dirty bandages.

Hobbs still managed to ruin himself with Sutherland. The way Adams put it together later, Hobbs found a black-beaded rosary on the ground between the supply dump and the latrines. The rosary was caked with mud, and its beads were tied in an ungainly series of knots, but Hobbs was sure it was the one that had belonged to Sergeant Devlin. So he rushed to find Sutherland who was collecting on a wager with one of the mess-hall sergeants. Sutherland's arms were full of cigarette cartons. And he was not happy to see C.D. Hobbs. When Hobbs offered him the rosary, he wouldn't take it.

"Not mine," he said. "Get the hell out of here."

But Hobbs insisted. He tried to wipe mud off a saint's medal because he thought the shined medal would prove to Sutherland that the rosary was his.

"Please, sir. You want this," he said. "I know you do." When Hobbs tried to lay the rosary across the lid of a cigarette carton, Sutherland detonated.

"That was in my pack, you little thief," he shouted, dropping his cigarettes so he could ready his fists. "You lifted it from my pack. I never took it out of there. I never lost it. You stole it, you fucking coward thief." It took Greenbaugh and two others to pull the former sergeant off Hobbs, who weathered one hard punch to the face before he flattened himself on the ground like a rug.

The rosary *was* Devlin's. There was no doubt about that. Everybody agreed. Yet nobody was able to get Sutherland to admit he'd seen or touched the thing since the day Devlin died. He refused to accept Devlin's absence. The old salts in the company knew what that meant. It meant Sutherland perceived the sergeant's death the only way he was capable of perceiving it— as a bad omen. And Sutherland made it his business to burn Hobbs to the ground from that moment on. The only enemy who deserved worse was the Chinese. "You listen to me," he told Adams, his face in a merciless twist. "MacArthur's put us in a noose made of Chinks, thousands of the godless bastards. Thousands. They'll take their toll before we get out of here. The way I see it, your buddy is part of the toll. He's weak, he'll pay, that's the way it's got to be with us and the Chinks. You better get used to the idea that your friend is the kind who slows you down and gets you captured. I saw it happen in Nanking. I had friends who were tortured into pieces, who were treated worse than hung meat, and I won't let it happen again. If that scum gets close to a front line while I'm a marine, I'll finish him myself."

Over the next three weeks, winter set in. The marines continued to move toward the Yalu River, crawling along the hip of the reservoir that lay like an unmarked scroll of light to the east. There was sporadic fighting, but the Chinese tended to melt off the hills in front of them. Adams did not believe the Chinese were retreating because they were whipped or scared. Sutherland wouldn't let him, or any of them, believe the Chinese were scared, although that was what the pogues who talked to the newspaper reporters liked to say.

Hill 1281 was just another anvil of Korean rock. Its crest

was all ice and wind-shorn granite, but the men of Easy Company tried to dig in because they had been ordered to do so. Every jolt of the pick jarred Adams's arm bones deep into his abused shoulder sockets. He was hungry but barely able to eat. And the Manchurian cold gnawed at his muscles until it took him twice as long as it should to accomplish the most meager tasks. Like digging a hole. Or taking a piss. He had to get his dick past more than four inches of layered clothing to take a piss, and it wasn't easy when his dick shrank up to a nub in the frigid clutch of the air. Then he didn't want to think about what was dripping out of him or look at it making a spoiled mark in the snow.

He tried to dig to the rhythm of sentences he'd read and re-read in the latest letter he'd received from his family. *We are praying for a wet winter,* his mother wrote, *though nothing too harsh for the yearlings. Charlotte does well at school, and with her music. She rides Jackson just as you asked. Gene is making plans to travel to the stock show in Denver after Christmas. He hopes to purchase a few Herefords for the meat.* He tried to dig his hole and listen to the sentences from home in a way that made him strong, not weak. *Please tell C.D. I saw his mother in Dixon when I visited with the Ladies' Aid Society. She mentions she will be moving to Encampment come spring. I have asked her to join us for a holiday celebration, but she does not yet know her plans. She sends her proud love to her son, as do I.*

Her son. Adams reckoned Posie Hobbs wouldn't be so proud of her son now, if she ever had been, which he doubted. Hobbs was no longer welcome among the gunners. Sutherland wouldn't have him in the unit. Only the cooks and the corpsmen would have him, which was maybe all right because, ever since Sergeant Devlin's death, C.D. had remained a pariah, the kind of hexed, bad-luck soldier nobody wanted to admit he knew.

Adams fumbled the clods of dirt he'd hacked free into a burlap bag. He could see Greenbaugh trying to do the same fifteen yards away, but even the sight of Greenbaugh didn't reduce his sense of solitude. Easy Company didn't have enough men to lug supplies up Hill 1281. They didn't have enough men to fill the holes and gun pits they were trying to dig. Illness and frost-bite had shredded their ranks. When he stood to tighten the parka hood that failed to protect his numb chin, he thought of the legendary Scottish clansman that Blue Pete Tosh used to tell stories about, the mad, loyal McKinney who froze to death on a highlands hilltop overlooking the storm-killed bodies of his sheep. *McKinney wouldnae leave his herd,* Blue Pete said, *not even when all were lost or dead.*

A hill like 1281 would suit Mad McKinney, Adams thought. Empty. Weather-bled. It was the kind of place a man could lose everything he cared about.

Then he saw Pilcher—skinny, unsteady Ry Pilcher. Pilcher was carrying the gun. Since Sudong, nobody but Sutherland was allowed to carry the gun.

Adams dropped his pick and went to meet Pilcher near the jury-rigged command post where the captain's men were splic-ing communications wire with their bare hands. They looked like children trying to tie shoelaces, the captain's men did, their fingers were so awkward and stiff. Hobbs should have had that job, Adams told himself. Hobbs should have done what Devlin asked him to do. He'd have a place—and some dignity—if he'd listened to Devlin. Instead, Hobbs had fallen into a bad crack of his own creation. Shaking his head, Adams started to offer Pilcher a cigarette, but the continuous cold ruined cigarettes now; it fractured the paper and tobacco into fragments that had no taste. So he offered nothing.

Pilcher's once-pink face was gray with malnutrition beneath the rind of his hood. But he still had a reckless, knowing smile framed by a pair of sharp canine teeth, and he was still able to laugh about the breaks that did or didn't come his way. The machine gun was on his back, wrapped in its tarpaulin and cloths.

"God damn Hill number 1-2-kiss-my-ass. They get steeper

every day." Pilcher wheezed as he spoke, his words cornered and tight. Adams felt the whistle in his own lungs as he listened to what he knew would be bad news. "You ain't gonna believe this. I wouldn't if I hadn't seen it myself. Suds is sent back. Lieutenant's orders." Pilcher loosened the muffler he wore over his mouth as he spoke. The muffler was bright gold and blue, the colors of his football team back home. It was so visible in the gray and green world in which they lived that Sutherland made him take it off whenever they were on the line.

"He give you the gun?" Adams couldn't believe Sutherland hadn't carried the gun uphill, lieutenant or no lieutenant. The gun was like a flag to Sutherland, a warning to the Chinese he hated, a sign that the struggling marines were nowhere near the end of their rope.

Pilcher's body wavered into what looked like a shrug. "Lieutenant told me to haul it up here after they arm-wrestled if off Suds. His breathing's real bad. He was going to his knees like a lung-shot hog."

Sutherland had been sick for days, chilled, coughing, but he wouldn't let the corpsmen touch him. Said he'd had the fucking malaria in the Philippines, the Japanese hadn't stopped for that, and he wasn't going to take some wounded son-of-a-bitching marine's place on a cot.

"They done hung us on the buck pole this time," Pilcher said, his smile in place but no feeling behind it. "Spoonhauer's got the platoon, you got the squad. I got nary a problem with that, but this hill is too big for us. Battalion thinks the Chinks won't do nothing, that we're buffaloing them by squatting up here like we're all high and mighty. Suds has got me thinking otherwise."

"We don't know what the Chinks will do." Adams spoke with the vehemence that had been stalking him for days, ever since he'd seen that Sutherland was sick. "We just need to get the gun ready. Somebody will decide what comes next."

Pilcher spat, or tried to. Adams knew they were both thinking the same thing: the time for sensible decisions was long past. He watched as the saliva that pooled on Pilcher's parka sleeve began to freeze. "Too damn cold for me to worry about it," Pilcher said. "Get shot up here, I won't even bleed."

"You won't have time to bleed," Adams said, thinking the Chinese were smart to let the weather do their job for them. "I'll be kicking your nuts up your spine for being so stupid."

Pilcher sniffed at the dry, frigid air as if there was a chance he'd smell something good, or at least important. "I didn't think it could get worse."

"It can always get worse."

"You sound like my mama. And all I'd like from her right now—or you—is a mess of dumplings baked with a big, fat, corn-fed hen. I could eat that meal every day of my life. When I get back, I just might."

They swung around, the gun anchored to Pilcher's bowed back, and they walked to where Adams had begun to construct the gun emplacement he was supposed to share with Sutherland. Now the pit was his. He looked over at Greenbaugh who was still scratching at his hole, rhythmically, blankly. That's how it was, he thought. Endurance was its own cruel victory. Every day they had less food, less shelter, less momentum. Soon, one side or the other would have nothing left to fight with or for.

He helped Pilcher ease the machine gun and its waxed garments to the ground. The sun was burning toward the end of its wick. There was too much left to do—a perimeter to clear, tripwire flares to string along the edge of their defenses. Adams stared at the bipod that was lashed to the back of his deflated field pack.

"You know what's got to happen, don't you? Now that you're practically a corporal."

Adams looked at Pilcher who was rewinding his hand-knit muffler. The mouth he covered was so skewed it looked mean.

"Get every marine you can. Don't stay in Suds's asshole and feel sorry for yourself. Don't wait for the captain to forget us again. Get Hobbs and Begnini on up here."

"He's no good for this," Adams said, thinking of Hobbs, his jaws locking around the words. "I don't want him here."

"He don't got to be good. He's just got to hold a gun and be on our side. That's all you can ask for."

"No. He's more trouble than he's worth." It was easy for him, simple, to shape the words that Sutherland would have shaped.

Pilcher's yellowed eyes went shrewd with pity. "Well, damn it all then. Whatever you say. But I wouldn't have picked you as one who didn't give a man his second chance."

Adams thought of the last time he'd actually spoken to Hobbs. C.D. didn't even pretend to muster with the squad anymore. They no longer ate or slept in the same tent. But they'd both been in one of the warming tents the evening before. The medical officers wanted the men to spend at least ten minutes of every two hours in a tent to reduce the effects of frostbite. The heat from the roaring stoves had felt like a salve to Adams, a thick blanket of comfort, even though his feet throbbed so hard with thawing pains that it was all he could do not to cry out. Then C.D. had ruined everything by approaching him and talking to him in jokes. "How you doing, Fremont? What about it?" His voice sounded clownish and shrill in the baked confines of the tent. "You think Old Etch would say it's cold enough for us out there? Or Gene? I can hear Uncle Gene telling how this is pussy work for men from Wyoming. Bad weather is what we own. We're used to this kind of cold."

"Nobody is used to this." Adams kept his eyes on his wooden feet because they made him feel hard-hearted. He didn't want to hear from Hobbs. He hated that Hobbs was saying things about the two of them in front of other men. He hated that his body was acknowledging pain. "Nobody should be used to this. Why don't you shut your mouth."

"But, Fremont, it's me talking. You don't. . . ." He never heard the end of Hobbs's sentence. C.D.'s voice was drowned out by the puling cough of the flu-ridden marine who sat between them. When Adams next raised his eyes in the murk of the tent, his friend was gone.

"I don't think C.D. would do us any good," he said to Pilcher, almost pleading. "He's used up."

"Ain't we all," Pilcher wheezed. "I just hope the same is true for the Chinks."

Sutherland had known how to do it. Sutherland had sampled them and raged at them and even blindsided them because Sutherland believed that hatreds were the only glues that held in the end. Hatred for the Communist Chinese. Hatred for niggling officers and the Tokyo command that served up marines like fodder. Hatred for the lack of supplies and ammunition. Sutherland believed all of those things had to smolder and burn within a man in order to make him fight. At his best, Sutherland reminded Adams of the ranch cook Basilio who had run so fierce and scorched at his job. Basilio had lasted at the Trumpet Bell for more than fifteen years until he suddenly began to steal things—belt buckles, spare socks, harmonicas— from the younger herders, Mexicans and Basques far beneath him in responsibility and age. Basilio had been sent away. Nobody offered an explanation for his sudden dishonesty except Old Etchepare who said that disgrace eventually came from heaven to all men.

Adams tried to fill another burlap bag with snow and dirt. The gun pit wasn't going to be finished before dark. And he was so tired. The news that Sutherland had been taken from them had brought on a dense, pressing need for sleep.

The wavering notes of a child's song echoed through his weariness.

"I'm working . . . on the railroad . . . just to pass . . . the time away."

The voice. The tune. They were so weirdly familiar. Adams spun to his left, then to his right, turning fast amid the freshly falling snowflakes that swept across the unfinished marine defenses like scraps of shredded paper.

". . . working on the railroad. . . ."

The constant, clawing wind brought tears to his eyes. His feet felt as if they belonged to another creature, something with thick and distant hooves. But he knew what he had heard. He knew that song from long, long ago. Hobbs was out there.

He found the man about one hundred yards to the north. Hobbs was chopping at the frozen earth with a dented entrenching tool as if he couldn't be stopped. Pilcher was nearby, admiring Hobbs's handiwork. It was clear to Adams that Pilcher had made it his business to reassign Hobbs to the squad. Greenbaugh had also joined the group, taking a break from his own futile digging. Greenbaugh was staring—half in worry, half in awe—at the machine-like consistency of Hobbs's digging.

"Be so cold tonight, we're gonna have to piss on the guns to keep 'em thawed. I thought we could use an extra pisser." Pilcher tried to wink one of his swollen eyes at Adams.

"Jesus," said Greenbaugh.

Hobbs halted his entrenching tool midswing and muttered a few words.

"Huh? What?" Just hearing the soft voice, especially its out-of-place yearning, upset Adams.

"Check your feet?"

He hadn't checked his feet, despite the captain's orders. He hadn't had time. None of them had. But he slid his mittens off for Hobbs, and his latest pair of gloves. His fingers were badly torn around the nails despite the application of gun grease. But they weren't blue. The sight of them cracked Hobbs's face with a strange smile.

"You're doing a good job there, C.D." Adams didn't know what else to say.

"Help you in the pit?" Hobbs asked. His irises were as mottled as storm clouds.

Adams stalled. Hobbs couldn't have asked a worse question. "I'll detail assignments after the flares are laid."

"What?" Greenbaugh straightened up. "You're going to keep him with you, aren't you?"

But Adams wasn't going to keep C.D. in the gun pit as his assistant. He couldn't risk it. He had to have somebody with glue.

"I said I'll square the assignments later."

"You just squared them." Greenbaugh showed Adams the underbelly of his eyes. "You're going to take Ry and stick me with *your* friend."

"Come on, Greenie. We're all in this together."

"Sure," said Greenbaugh. "And I'm in it with *that*." He pointed his shovel blade at Hobbs who had removed his own gloves and was using his fingers to harvest the snot icicles that hung above his lip. He was eating them.

"Knock it off, C.D."

Hobbs gave some quick yips, almost like a collie's.

"Fuck," said Greenbaugh.

"I'll work on it," Adams said.

Hobbs whispered something into the palm of his bare hand.

"What?" hissed Adams, feeling bewildered and besieged.

Hobbs bit into his hand, then he took a hard, immobile look at each of the three men. He pointed over their aligned shoulders. "Somebody wants a ride on the railroad."

"Jesus. He's a complete loon." Greenbaugh dropped his shovel.

"Just to pass the time of day."

Adams was still trying to decipher the words that had come from the dry sieve of Hobbs's vocal chords when Pilcher stopped him. Pilcher was staring east, toward Chosin Reservoir. The weather had cleared for a moment. The falling sun bathed the neighboring array of hills in a warm, golden light. Basking in that light was rank upon rank of neatly assembled soldiers. Every hill they could now see was thatched with waiting Chinese.

Adams looked at his watch dial. The captain had put the company on 50 percent alert, so Pilcher lay curled behind him in an arrested state that might be called sleep. It was Adams's first rotation on watch, and all he knew for certain was that the sky had become a wide-mouthed kettle filled with an endless, purifying cold. The moisture in his breath froze and fell upon the flanges of the gun like the chaff of stars. There was fighting to the west. He could hear the battle sounds and see the toylike flash of distant mortars and the tiny pendants of the flares. The Chinese were no longer hiding in their caves or wherever it was they hid when the spotter planes looked for them during the day. They'd revealed themselves before sunset. They appeared prepared to attack. He remembered what Devlin—prowling, questing Devlin—had told them just before they'd chivvied up to march toward the Yalu. Devlin said, "There's only one road to this Chosin and the river. If I'm the gook general, I use every night I got trying to cut that road."

It was time to rouse Pilcher. They both needed to change their socks. He peered across the patchwork of rock and dirt and snow toward Hobbs and Greenbaugh's hole. Hobbs liked to have help with his shoe pacs. He'd told Greenbaugh that, how Hobbs might need a little help with his feet. Greenbaugh was a good squad member, but Adams suspected it would be a long time before Greenbaugh did anything extra to take care of C.D. Hobbs.

He shook Pilcher awake. Once sleep overtook a man on Hill 1281, if it did, it was difficult to convince that man to come back into his suffering body. He unzipped Pilcher's sleeping bag and shoved it from his shoulders. Then he whispered to Pilcher to grab onto his rifle. He couldn't see anything except a pale medallion of skin above the light and dark stripes of Pilcher's knotted muffler, but his assistant was moving.

He crawled out of his own bag, which had been zipped to the waist, and began to unlace his knee-high shoe pacs. The pacs were warm, but not ventilated. This meant they had to keep changing their socks or their feet might freeze solid in their own moisture. He drew his extra socks from the front of his wool overpants, cursing how awkward he felt. He was so cold he couldn't coordinate his arms with his legs. When he yanked his shoe pacs off, his teeth began to chatter until his jaw rang with their tune.

Pilcher wasn't doing so well, either. He'd slept with his pacs off, which was good for reducing moisture but bad if a fight started in a hurry. Guys had lived through firefights like that, bootless, only to hear a surgeon tell them they were going to lose their feet. That's what Hebert, the corpsman, said. Hebert

was always bugging them about their feet. Adams signaled to
Pilcher, with his teeth ground together, that he'd help him with
his laces when he needed it.

Pilcher nodded. He was still groggy, but he pulled his feet
clear of his bag. He fished a pair of socks from beneath the coil
of his muffler and handed them to Adams. Adams tried to work
fast, priding himself on any remnant of dexterity. He pulled
off Pilcher's socks, one by one, as he cradled both bony heels
in his lap. He was about to massage Pilcher's toes—captain's
orders—when he realized strips of skin had peeled away from
Pilcher's feet with his socks. There was a smell, too, one he recognized above the shared rankness of sweat and smeared shit.
The sweetness of rot. He did what he could with Pilcher's toes,
drew on the fresh socks, then shoved the feet into the cold, dry
shoe pacs. He worked the stiff laces through the eyelets and up
the length of Pilcher's ankles and calves. Pilcher needed to go
to the aid tent at first light. But Adams wasn't going to tell him
that now.

He looked again across the ransacked fifteen yards to the
other hole. No shadows. No stirring. But they couldn't be doing
well. Nobody could be, not a Chink peasant or an American
marine. He watched Pilcher work himself onto his knees. The
other man was sobbing under the layers of his shirts and coats.
That's what it took, weeping. The machine gun rested above
them, its barrel pointing into emptiness. The damn thing might
not even work at twenty degrees below zero. Sutherland had,
just that morning, lubricated the gun with powder because no
version of oil or grease or even hair tonic was trustworthy in
these temperatures. But Sutherland hadn't said what to do if
the gun wouldn't fire. He hadn't acted like it was a possibility.

Adams wasn't sure it mattered. The gun was the base of fire
for their scraggly segment of the line. If the gun went down,
they would all surely go down with it.

Two a.m. He was back on watch after an hour when his mind
had squatted in a gray and murky place without moving. When

Pilcher slapped him into consciousness, the first thing he recognized was a swollen tongue that tasted of bloody rags. His
tongue. He sucked some chlorinated water from the ice block
of his canteen and gave the high sign to the lieutenant who
was making his rounds. Pilcher crawled back into his bag. So
Adams was among the first to hear them, the hundreds and
hundreds and hundreds of footsteps that ground the crusted
snow to powder.

Footsteps. He squinted into the killing wind that blew down
the barrel of the gun. His eyes shed solid tears. Footsteps,
marching. Then came the sound of a Chinese officer singing
cadence. His voice was a ghost voice, alone and echoing, and
it soared toward Adams's ears like a dark and ravenous bird.
"Nobody live forever. You die! Nobody live forever. You die!"
A ghost voice in English. Adams felt himself shrink into the
close harbor of his clothes.

Ten divisions of seasoned soldiers. That's what the prisoners
at Sudong had promised. And Easy Company was defending
Hill 1281 with fewer than two hundred men.

Here they come.
Here they come.
Here they come.

Warnings rose from hole to hole, then throttled themselves
to whispers. Adams took one hand off the gun and pressed
his helmet down onto his head as Pilcher kicked clear of his
bag. Adams made himself swivel and move, made himself force
moisture down his mistreated throat. The ammunition belts
were ready. He had a pistol, a few grenades. He couldn't see
a god damn thing yet, only hear them, god damn the Chinese
for being so ready for this terrain and temperature. Was Pilcher
ready? He elbowed Pilcher in the thickness of his upper arm.
He felt the solid brace of Pilcher's feet and the full flex of his
tendons as if they were his own.

Then he heard something else, a thin thread of music spinning itself below the Chinese officer's taunt. "No-bo-dy-live-
you-die. No-bo-dy-live-you-die!" There was another song in the

air. "Dinah, won't you blow? Dinah, won't you blow? Dinah, won't you blow your h-h-horn?" Adams's chest went as numb as his face. He knew exactly where the song was coming from.

He didn't even think about it. He just left Pilcher and the gun. He rolled up and over the pitiful sandbags not filled with sand, then crawled left on the blunt points of his elbows and knees. The jitters, the shakes—they all had them. But he couldn't let Hobbs go full shatter now. He couldn't. He was the one responsible. *Don't do it,* he shouted into the endless cavern of his own head, *Don't sing so they can find us. Don't make that god damn noise.* He knew if Sutherland had been there, he would have slit C.D. Hobbs's throat without a thought.

He jackknifed into the hole where Greenbaugh was crouched at the front rim, a still life of watchfulness and horror. Hobbs was cross-legged in the black bottom of the hole, invisible except for the bobbing white root of his head. He'd taken off his helmet and hats. Adams grabbed for the handle of Hobbs's parka hood. As they touched, he was filled with a roaring, insatiable anger that seemed to come from a deep, craving place far below his wished-for discipline. *You are not worth it.* Those were the words that came to him as he blindly struck out at Hobbs again and again and again. Anger. Sutherland's glue. He struck at Hobbs's mouth because it was so unprotected and moving. *You'll get us killed.* He felt the notches of Hobbs's teeth. He felt the puniness of Hobbs's wagging neck.

That puniness so infuriated him that he reached into the pocket that held the honed Baker knife he'd kept since he was a boy. He would do it if he had to, he really would. He would make Hobbs be quiet. He whispered savagely to Hobbs that he had to stop singing, but Hobbs didn't stop. It was as though he wanted to be saved from his own uselessness. The wish was right there in the quivering nakedness of his eyes. It was in the tuneless chime of his voice. Adams clamped a hand over Hobbs's moving mouth, but Hobbs kept singing. As Adams opened the blade of the Baker knife, something black and smooth brushed across his vision, and he believed he saw Hobbs tilt his jaw upward to give him and his blade a better angle.

The thunk, thunk, thunk of the marine mortars surprised him. The illumination rounds went up first, and they backlit the human warp and weft that was about to blanket Easy Company: thousands of Chinese soldiers in perfect ranks, more than Adams had imagined in his worst, elastic nightmares. "You die! You die!" The Chinese officer exhorted his men while Adams watched the knife waver in his enraged hand. He backed away from Hobbs. But his intentions slipped slender and sharp into his blood like an inoculation. He should have felt fear as he lay exposed beneath the fading flares of the battlefield, but he didn't. He was not afraid. What he felt was a greedy resilience, a hurtling desire to stand straight up so the Chinese could see him. *Come at me, you bastards. I'm here.* It was as if everything that had once thrived within Hobbs and within himself had blended into a tensile, mocking anger. Hobbs became invisible to him. Hobbs was forgotten. He recognized nothing inside himself except Sutherland's admonition: *Don't let them take you alive.*

Then. Trip flares fountained all along their front. There were bugle blasts. Torrents of cursing. Shouting. There were Chinese whistle shrieks that became blue flames inside his ears. He never remembered crawling back to his position, though he remembered Pilcher's face, how Pilcher's eyes were blistered with the acid wash of betrayal. He had to shove Pilcher out of the gunner's position where he'd settled himself in sacrifice. He had to make them both believe that he was rock solid again. They began to fire, late, and the gun was sluggish in the cold, but they reaped the shadows that moved toward them, rank by rank. Their muzzle belched its bright orange flame of invitation. The grenadiers would come for them very soon. That was how the Chinese targeted a machine gun.

Mortars began to plummet into their lines, sizzling dirt and ice, and there was flash after flash from the poorly made Chinese concussion grenades that blinded them for a second or two but inevitably fell short. Pilcher linked belt after belt of ammunition as they swept the field, pivoting from stake to stake, cross-stitching their tracers with the red lines from

Spoonhauer's faraway gun. There were so many Chinese. Marine mortars shoveled the parading men into waist-high piles, and still they came, the men from the rear picking up the weapons of the fallen. When Pilcher unpinned a grenade, Adams knew some of the Chinese were finally getting through, getting closer. Which was why neither of them saw Hobbs fish-flopping out of his hole.

Then the gun stopped. It stuttered only once, its barrel steaming like the back of an exhausted animal, before it coughed up a last licking tongue of flame. Pilcher released the belt and cleared the firing mechanism, but the gun wasn't jammed, and they both knew it. There was still covering fire from Spoonhauer's squad, so they tried again, but the gun was down—too hot, too cold, or both.

He set Pilcher above him with an M1 and several clips. He was supposed to keep his hands covered, but he had no choice. He took the trigger housing off before he removed his gloves because he didn't want to touch the gun's cooked metal until he had to. Then he stripped off his gloves and put the flashlight he kept in his pants pocket between his teeth. Except the flashlight, too, had frozen. With nerveless fingers he felt blindly for the pin he suspected had been bent by the torque of the firing mechanism. He found it. If the ruined pin burned his fingertips, he couldn't feel it.

The air above them was torn with riptides of light, and there was more noise than his ears could hear. Pilcher hovered over him, saying something with his blackened face.

Okay, Adams signed. He understood. The line was fraying, and they needed more covering fire to give them time to put a new pin in the gun. Pilcher would go get more men. He mouthed three words to Adams. *Wait for me.*

Adams nodded. And he drew the German pistol he'd bought in Wonsan.

Pilcher rose from his rabbit hunter's crouch, his M1 jumping like a compass needle. But, after just a few steps, he stumbled. He seemed to leap in the direction of Greenbaugh's hole as if he meant to leap, then he collapsed into a scrap of shadow.

His frozen feet, that's what Adams wanted it to be. He wanted Pilcher to stand up after tripping on his frozen feet. But Pilcher never moved. Adams felt Pilcher's rise and fall in the parabola of his own pulse. He swung his unholstered pistol and shot into the blunt muzzle fire of a Chinese burp gunner. He fired until his clip was empty. When he hunkered to reload, he realized the long, toneless screech in his ears was his own.

He wasn't going to last long by himself, so he began to feel it again—the greed for living he'd felt when he'd beaten Hobbs, when he'd begun to sense it was his own brutal clarity of purpose that had summoned the Chinese. Some men were weak, some were strong. Some men were meant to be outnumbered. He was counting his grenades by touch when a dark shape tried to lizard itself into the back of his hole. He cocked his pistol even as his bones filled with a venomous thrill. It would be Sutherland. That was only right. Sutherland had risen from the aid tent and yanked the needles out of his arms and thundered up that godforsaken hill to help him, to tell him what to do.

But it wasn't Sutherland. It was Hobbs.

Bald, bloody-mouthed, twitching like a broken-backed dog that's found its ditch: it was Hobbs. His uniform was plastered with substances that were moist and clumped. His mouth hung wide open. Adams kept his pistol raised. He wasn't sure he recognized the man in his sights.

Hobbs was sledding a fat Browning Automatic behind him, dragging it like it was a piece of salvaged timber. Adams knew the B.A.R. was a precious opportunity; it was a weapon he could use, yet he kept himself from snatching at the gun. He didn't want to be rushed by hope, not ever again. And he didn't want responsibility for Hobbs. He turned and fired an unconsidered clip from his pistol into the area his machine gun was supposed to cover. The Chinese had, for the moment, backed out of range.

"He, he, he, he." Hobbs stiff-armed the B.A.R., trying to angle it against his legs like a crutch. And he was saying something, or trying to. A close mortar drop blew pulverized rock into the air, and while Adams swiped a hand across his face, tasting blood and cinder, he saw that Hobbs had barely flinched. His eyes were melted wide open.

Adams made himself reach out for the other man, his friend. He waited for the electric hatred to spark again between them, but he didn't feel it this time, he felt something watery and dwindling instead. Hobbs's body tilted into his own, and it became as shapeless as a wool sack, the great canvas kind they'd filled at the Cow Creek shearing sheds when they were young. He probed Hobbs's neck for a pulse, his belt and pockets for ammunition. Hobbs was alive, but he carried nothing with him, not even a bandage. It was as if he'd been picked clean.

Rifle fire increased along the line. The Chinese, Adams guessed, had finally found a weak point. They would gush through it like oil. He touched his last two grenades, then rubbed the Browning as if to give it some life. *One more genie, one last bottle.* The words came to him in Sutherland's blunt, currentless voice. He rested the gun across his thighs and reached forward to slip the hood of Hobbs's parka over his shaved and naked head. Hobbs had come back to him, the saboteur, the fool. He'd nearly ruined everything, and then he'd tried to bring some kind of salvation to Adams, as if there was anything left on that damnable hill that might save either one of them.

"He, he, he, he." Hobbs's gashed mouth continued to gulp around a single syllable. Adams tried to prop him in the deepest portion of the pit. It was, he thought, the same as being alone.

He swung the B.A.R. over the pale crown of burlap bags. As soon as he sighted movement, he pulled the Browning's trigger and fired a short burst. That marked him, by damn. He could see white-clad figures duckwalking toward Greenbaugh's position, which now lay quiet and smoldering. The Chinese would get to him next. He felt a sifted desire to say something final to C.D., something clear and practical formed from the boyhood lives that were all that would ever give their disposable bodies a name. But he didn't know what the right words might be. As he scanned the landscape in front of him, he saw the first flowers of a white phosphorus barrage bloom their way uphill. The barrage was on a line with their gun pit. Adams thought about the white fire of the winter sun over Bell Butte. He thought about the red petals of his guts blossoming on a slab of Korean ice. He fired the last few bullets in the Browning, then dropped it. *Come and get me, then.* There was no reason to hide anymore. *Thousands of the bastards.* They needed to know who he was before they killed him, who he'd tried to be. *Not taken alive.* But when he tried to stand tall in the gun pit, when he tried to make himself into a target they'd remember, he got snagged. Tripped. Thwarted. He was flattened onto the cartridge-covered bottom of the pit. *Let me go, damn it, you need to let me go.* Those were the only words he could scream into his mouth as the coward C.D. Hobbs grappled the two of them together, and the world they knew went flat and scorched and bright.

Adams pried himself out of the ground. His eyes and lungs were seared shut from smoke. He didn't know who he was, where he was. Blind, deaf, spinning in an inferno. He would never know the name of the marine who dragged him to the aid station. The man did not have a face, only the steady, out-of-place strength of a plow horse. The same man carried Hobbs, peeled and burning, off the line and left him with the over-whelmed corpsman who was manning a makeshift aid station on the backside of the hill. The corpsman, whose name was Wade, shed tears as he worked. Adams remembered this. The corpsman was sheltered from the wind by a wall of dead ma-rines, his forearms were jellied with frozen blood, the Chinese were shelling the hilltop, and he was down to his last ampule of morphine. He wept tears of terrible frustration. But when he saw that Hobbs's stomach hadn't been ripped open by the blast, he stuck that final ampule into his own blackened mouth so the painkiller inside it would thaw.

"Hold him hard," he ordered Adams as he struggled with Hobbs's clothes looking for an unfried patch of skin. Adams held Hobbs hard. He gave Wade the Baker knife. The blade

was slim and sharp, and the corpsman slashed an opening in
Hobbs's smoking parka. Adams watched plummeting flakes of
snow melt against Hobbs's melted skin while Hobbs bucked
and writhed until the morphine made his pain unreal. "Get
him out of here," the corpsman shouted, "while you've got a
chance." And Adams tried to get them out of there. But his
numbed feet would not allow him to walk upright. He dragged
himself and Hobbs to the base of a thorny bush. It was as far
as he could go. He curled under the branches of the bush like a
wounded pup and waited for his own tears.

Here they come.

Here they come.

But no one came for him.

Nobody walked or crawled off Hill 1281 until the next morning. That's the story the marines would tell. The whole damn
position had been surrounded. The Americans, outnumbered a
dozen to one, fought with their rifle butts and fists until dawn.

But a stretcher bearer somehow came for Hobbs, creeping
through the smoke and the night, a stretcher bearer who looked
familiar and who worked alone. Adams asked the corpsman,
Wade, if he knew the marine with the reddish beard and the
rosary wrapped in his bandolier, but the corpsman was dead
from a shrapnel wound to the neck. He could not answer
Adams's questions. Neither could the reinforcements from Able
Company, the ones who poked at him with their frosted bayonets because they assumed he was dead and rigged with booby
traps. It was a new day then, an hour of bloodless silence in the
cold. The first slow spill of sunlight chastened itself behind the
scrim of winter. The dead were laid out in rows. Adams hob-
bled off Hill 1281 on the arms of marines who looked older
than any men he'd even seen. He had been spared. His friend
was gone, no one knew how or when. He and Hobbs, all of
Easy Company, all of America's army, had been severed by the
jaws of Chosin.

Trumpet Bell Land & Sheep Company

Baggs, Wyoming

1975

AUGUST WAS SWELTERING. THE ENTIRE MONTH WAS AN unbroken invasion of heat and crickets. And Charlotte gave them no warning. She hitchhiked from San Francisco to Wamsutter on the interstate, then caught a ride south with a road-survey crew that politely drove her all the way to the front door of the house. Charlotte found Maria Delores in the kitchen scrubbing a skillet. During her years away from the ranch, Charlotte had developed a skeptical attitude about her brother's romantic activities. She assumed Maria was Adams's latest short-time woman, and she began to act badly. She spoke Spanish well enough to offend Maria Delores a dozen different ways, so when Adams finally came in from the fields with Hobbs and Maria's husband, Omero, all of them in high rubber boots flecked with the legs and wings of interfering crickets, Maria removed her apron and went to sit in her husband's quarter-ton truck. The three men immediately understood it was their duty to repair the invisible damage they smelled in the air that also smelled of the tortillas and beef and beans laid out for lunch.

Adams began by embracing his sister. "I don't believe it," he said, surprise and an unexpected wariness mixing in the capsule of his chest. "I don't believe what I'm seeing." Hobbs embraced Charlotte too. Then Adams introduced the silent Omero, saying that he and Maria Delores were lifesavers since it was hay season and a very busy time on the ranch.

Charlotte was clearly mortified by her mistake, though she fought the embarrassment that striped her face and made no apology for it. Adams could see she wasn't ready to admit that her tangled feelings about coming home to the Trumpet Bell had already led her to be cruel.

99

He said, "I am amazed. Why don't you sit down with us, have some lunch." It wasn't in him to postpone an afternoon of work just because Charlotte had turned up with a stuffed seaman's bag stenciled with the name of some pawnshop sailor. Even though he hadn't seen her in a couple of years, he wasn't going to chase after her with special treatment. They all sat at the chrome-legged kitchen table, and Adams served the lunch, except to Charlotte who swore she wasn't hungry. They ate in silence until Hobbs started in with his questions.

"How was your trip, Charlotte? Did you see a lot of rain?" Charlotte said she hadn't been rained on.

"Did you leave things good in sunny California? Are the oranges out there ripe to eat? Did you stop to visit the ocean?"

They were plain, inoffensive questions uttered between damp swallows of tortilla and milk, accompanied by Hobbs's cheerfully bobbing head, but Adams would later wonder if it got away from him right there at that first meal. Was Charlotte so stung by her mistake with Maria Delores that she shied toward Hobbs like a spooked filly? Did C.D. know what he was reaching for when he reached out to Charlotte? Maybe what happened later wouldn't have happened if they both had been more alert. Maybe Charlotte would have reserved her sharpest knives for him and for Buren, her brothers, which seemed to be her intention at the time.

They finished the lunch and left the dishes stacked near the sink before going to the porch to have cigarettes. Hobbs mentioned that Charlotte's old bay horse, Redrock, was still alive, and he introduced Charlotte to the pair of collies, Nan and Sol, who were lolling in the slim shade of the house. Nan and Sol were in some half-remembered way descended from the dogs Charlotte had known as a girl.

"I'm glad you've got good dogs," she said, her smile finally relaxing into a genuine curve.

Adams found himself watching her as he gave her one of his cigarettes. She had the freckled, kid-glove skin of their mother, the kind of skin that retained a fine array of wrinkles around the mouth and eyes but never lost its shine. Her red-blond hair had given up the curl of childhood and now lay sleek against her small skull. She wore the hair long, bound at her neck in a clasp of turquoise and silver. There was lots of jewelry on one wrist—most of it strings of simple, colored beads—and none on the other. Adams admired his sister's layers of cotton vests and skirts, especially the blues and purples that deepened the pale concentration of her upturned eyes.

She had been married in California, he had even met her husband once, but he thought her arrival at the Trumpet Bell might mean the husband was out of the picture. It didn't matter. He would accept whatever stories she chose to tell about herself. He would help her if she asked for help. The uneasiness he'd felt at her arrival was what he always felt prior to a change of some sort. Charlotte was his sister, the undeterred creature who had once followed him to every far-flung corner of the ranch and placed on him her earnest, sometimes petulant, demands. Her years as a teacher in California might have reshaped her in some ways, but he sensed the woman he saw in front of him would still be difficult to deny.

He said, "You can set up in your old room. Maria Delores can get you some sheets. It should be fairly clean in there."

She said, "I'll handle it. I won't bother anybody with extra work. I'm not exactly a guest." She smiled and patted the wrist above his work-harrowed hand. She left her hand on his as she ground her cigarette into the wooden planks of the porch with her rope-soled sandal.

When the three men returned from the fields later that evening, they could see Charlotte had been working with the horses. One of them, Redrock, was still wet from exercise. Maria Delores was back in her husband's truck, but that wasn't unusual. She often waited there for Omero at the end of the day. Adams went to his own truck and took from his cowhide wallet the money he owed Omero and Maria Delores plus cash for the next week's groceries.

"We done good today," he said to Omero as he handed off the tight fold of bills. "I don't think my sister meant to be such a surprise."

Omero and Maria Delores nodded, their faces guarded and polite.

"I appreciate your help on the groceries, Maria. I'll make sure you're queen of the kitchen from now on."

Maria touched her neck just above the collarbone. "Gracias, Señor."

"Gracias to the two of you for getting us through the day."

The couple drove out the drive and headed south toward a trailer Adams owned near Piney Butte. Although Adams had offered to move the trailer closer to headquarters, Omero hadn't accepted the offer. He and Maria Delores liked their privacy. Now that Charlotte had arrived in all her glory, Adams thought the arrangement might be for the best.

Charlotte was in the kitchen stirring a pot of soup that had clearly been made by Maria Delores. Her presence at the stove was exaggerated proof of a truce that may or may not have been negotiated on both sides. She wore jeans with a long-sleeved gingham shirt and her old calfskin 4-H boots, and both Hobbs and Adams stopped in the doorway to look at her. She was backlit by the sifted light of evening. The sight of her in those clothes, standing in that place, threw them back into the first third of their lives. They had been her caretakers once. That ancient fact was almost impossible to reconcile with what they saw in front of them. Charlotte laughed at their hesitation and promised she hadn't actually cooked the soup. "If you're not ready to eat, let's fire up some cigarettes and get to know each other again."

They sat on the porch—on the steps rather than the pine bench, which was covered with tire chains and axe handles and other tools that kept themselves close at hand—and they talked for a long time while they smoked. The dogs settled intermittently at their feet, watchful of the newcomer as herd dogs always are. Charlotte told them about her life on the West Coast.

"I stayed with Elon as long as I could," she said. "I still love his politics. He's a rampaging idealist, and I like that because

I'm not. But Elon is always raising the bar—on me and everybody else. When we were in Mexico, he told me he'd stopped
believing in marriage."

"You ain't married?" Hobbs looked up from his seat on the
lowest step.

"Not anymore." Charlotte whistled a high note to herself.
"Right now I'm as independent and unhindered as you boys.
Hell, I might even be more ignorant."

"You give up the school teaching?" Adams held the smoke
from his cigarette tight in his mouth.

"For a while, maybe. But don't worry, I got money."

"Your money's no good here," Adams said. "No reason to
mention it."

"I got money," Charlotte said again. "What I don't have is
friends. Not the ones in Frisco, not the ones south of the border. They all stayed with Elon or they split. Bullshitters. They
didn't stick to anything they said they believed in."

Adams watched his sister's foot patter into a nervous tap
against the porch step. Charlotte's friends hadn't held up. Her
life wasn't holding up. He wondered if she'd come home to see
if California was a world she could do without.

"What should they believe in, them friends who went away?"
Hobbs's voice skidded across its consonants the way it did when
he talked to weaned lambs.

Charlotte chuckled, sharp and defensive. "They should believe in what I believe in—moving on. I believe in making things
work for me. I took Red for a slow ride toward the Butte while
you all were working. That old horse isn't up to much, but it
felt good to cross that land again."

"Feels good to have you back," Hobbs said, and he said
it so fast and so without shading they all three laughed. The
words should have been Adams's.

"We'll take you any way you come—"

"—as long as I do my share of chores. I know how your
mind works, big brother. Don't worry. I still remember how
to hoist a shovel." And they all laughed again. Charlotte held

up a hand for another smoke, and Adams saw she'd taken the beaded jewelry off her wrist. He gave her the cigarette.

"You two amaze me," she said, "living out here as if it's the 1940s with Uncle Gene hounding your asses at every turn. It's like nothing's changed."

"Ranching's changed a lot." Hobbs leaped in again, using his mouth for words that should have been Adams's. "Margins is tight on sheep. Most of the good money these days is in cows." Adams felt himself pull back from the conversation, sensing the razor edge of a need in Charlotte's words. His sister was after something that had nothing to do with how dull he and Hobbs were or the dullness of the ranch. It seemed important that he figure out what that need was.

"The air still stinks the same. Nothing but dry rot and dust," she said.

Hobbs responded to Charlotte's comment as if she couldn't be serious. He smiled in silence.

Adams decided to nudge his sister right back. "Maybe you'd like to tend camp for me in the Madres. I need somebody tough up there the last two weeks of this month." He stood and stretched his arms above his head. It was his signal they should go inside.

"Fuck you, brother. Sheep are boring. You know how I feel about them. I can do more good by staying right here." Charlotte gave him a grin laden with prankishness and irritation before she unfurled her palm for yet another smoke. He tossed her the pack and left the two of them on the porch.

They came to the table a few minutes later, and Adams stopped eating long enough to serve them from the soup pot and a plate of sliced bread. He watched as Charlotte made a point of pretending she was conspiring with Hobbs. She whispered and gestured to C.D. in an attempt to continue the conversation they'd begun outside, but Hobbs didn't return the whispers. He didn't know how to primp and scheme. He was so happy to have Charlotte in the house where they'd been kids together that he failed to follow her lead.

So Charlotte tried a different tack. "Tell me about what you've done since I saw you last, C.D. Where you've been."

"Well." Hobbs hesitated, sneaking a sideways glance at Adams. "Well. I got fired by this manager for Portaco. He didn't like me."

"That was near Tulsa," Adams added, though he didn't tell Charlotte the Portaco oil-field incident had in fact occurred several years before. Hobbs had lost a lot of jobs over the years, and he had trouble with timelines when he got nervous.

"Tulsa," Hobbs nodded. "In Oklahoma. I never have much luck in Oklahoma. They got a excellent hospital there, though. I have been in that hospital."

Adams watched Charlotte roll her blue eyes with manufactured sympathy as if she knew the hell and drudgery of hospitals. Which she most certainly did not. Charlotte had never visited Hobbs in the musty, cackling veterans ward where he'd had to spend a great deal of time after the war. She'd been too young. Their mother thought the experience would upset her.

"But you're not in a hospital now," she said, smiling expansively. "You look good to me. What's the best thing that's happened to you recently? What's been exciting?"

Hobbs pretended to rub his unshaved jaw in complete concentration. Then he winked at Charlotte as if he finally understood her game. "Fremont," he said. "Everything the way it is right here."

Charlotte's cheeks flushed pink. "Oh, come on. There's got to be more than that."

"There's not," insisted Hobbs, and Adams watched him push his shaky left hand out onto the table, a thing he did when he became agitated.

"I don't get it, C.D. You just about waste your whole life by getting killed in Korea, which nobody would do now because they don't buy that U.S. imperial crap. Then you get better, and you keep wasting your life. Why don't you elevate yourself a few million feet above where you're stuck in my brother's sheep shit and see what you're really about, what's happening in the real world? Hanoi? Do you know what we did there? Watergate? This is not the real world. Look at what they fucking did to you and your face in that pathetic 'police action.' You ought to be in court demanding compensation."

Hobbs drew his hands to his sides and took on the tense, hunched posture of a prey animal that was somehow compelled to wait for its attacker to strike again. For Adams, the room became airless, choking. He knew Charlotte could be bossy and dramatic, but he had failed to see this coming, this ricocheting quest for pain. He had been sure Charlotte would respect the twenty-five-year-old rule of not talking about the war. Everybody else did. He'd allowed her to lecture him and Hobbs about their bachelor isolation on the ranch. That was tolerable. Charlotte was dislocated and young and hungry for more interesting prospects, which she would surely find. But to talk about Hobbs's wounds in any way other than the way she'd talked about them in 1951 was a serious betrayal. Eleven-year-old Charlotte Adams had written C.D. Hobbs at least one cheerful letter a week while he was having his surgeries in Japan. She had greeted him—and his disturbing scars— with simple affection when he was finally shipped home. She had not seen Hobbs regularly after that, no one had, but she had always accepted him. She had always been a comfort. To change her tune now, to suggest that Hobbs had indeed been disfigured, was beyond forgiveness.

"Charlotte." Adams tried not to shout as he felt something anchor itself among his tightened ribs, a thing with talons and jaws. "You need to put a lid on it right now. You need to recall what the situation is here."

Charlotte half-raised herself from her chair, stopped, then raised herself completely to push away from the chrome-legged table. She stood as Hobbs's red mouth wrestled with the syllables *no no no* of a black and private denial. She stepped backward as his spasmed hand tore at the scarred stump of his ear. Adams, too, witnessed the familiar signs of stress. They made his skin prickle and burn. "Oh . . . no," Charlotte said in a high echo of Hobbs's own cries. "Oh god, C. D. . . . I was just trying to . . . I didn't mean . . . I'm so sorry." And she fled the table for the empty rooms upstairs where Adams heard the hard pacing of her boots against the ceiling for a long time before there was silence.

Charlotte was as good as her word when it came to ranch work. She woke up early. She helped Maria fix breakfast and lunch. She was a bale-lifting maniac in the hay fields. She even went up the road to help the neighbors, Steve and Nod Barnheisel, take in their hay when the Trumpet Bell's was all stored. Nod Barnheisel offered to sell her his quarter-horse colt because Redrock had gotten so old, but Charlotte told Nod that she didn't expect to be on the ranch long enough to do justice to a good colt. It was the same reason she gave when she refused Nod's invitation to dinner and a movie. Adams decided his little sister had been shocked into good behavior. He didn't believe it was in her nature to be mean to people as she'd been mean to Hobbs. California might have accustomed her to a brand of ferocity that was less common in Wyoming, but it was his experience that summer at the Trumpet Bell brought out the best in people. The long, bright days, the redeeming scents of grass and water—these always made his life seem as vivid and whole as the spinning blue disc of the sky.

Charlotte also did other deeds that impressed her brother. She attended services at the old church in Savery. She called on their neighbors, most of whom still lived in the log and plank houses where they had raised their families. Charlotte didn't say much about these visits except to list the gifts she'd been given by Portia Adams's grateful friends—the dripping honeycombs, the wine-bright jars of chokecherry jam, the bouquets of sunflowers. She took pains not to exhibit the righteousness that had flamed within her when she first arrived home. Adams suspected the focus and efficiency he now saw in his sister was what her students in California saw: Charlotte was a woman of sure, gripping affections. And she had energy to spare. He

began to imagine what the next few months would be like, the
interesting times they might have, if she decided to stay on the
ranch through the winter.

Buren was the one who broke the news, a task he performed
with exacting pleasure. It was a Sunday morning, late. Buren,
long divorced from his first and only wife, had driven over
from Cheyenne where he now worked for the governor to see
Charlotte, whom he regarded with the world-weary detach-
ment of a distant cousin. He and Adams were drinking coffee in the ranch yard. Buren wore a borrowed pair of irrigator
boots to preserve the cuffs of his trousers. They, in turn, were
watched by a pair of bead-eyed magpies that sat on the corral fence ready to scavenge anything the brothers might throw
their way.

"You *do* know what they're doing, don't you?" Buren spoke
without prelude. He held his lit cigarette at the end of his fingers, its tip sheltered from a light breeze by the pillar of his
thigh. His face was lean and angular in the morning sun,
almost handsome except for the sallow tinge of his eyes. "I
caught them *in flagrante,* as they say—quite early this morning.
They've been using your shed."

Adams didn't dare look at his brother. He stared at the stark
plumage of the magpies instead, suddenly peeved by the cock-
ade elegance of their long tails. They were useless birds. They
enjoyed pecking the eyes out of his sick lambs when they could
beat the ravens to the job.

"So?" He tried to throw Buren's superior indifference back
in his face. He hoped a display of false impatience would cover
his panic.

"So, we're all too old to suggest the act is actually indecent
even though C.D. is the next best thing to a . . . brother."

"You're a sick bastard, if you don't mind my saying." Adams
tried to focus on his brother's ramrod posture and the absence
of sympathy that hoisted his words onto a high platform of
gloating. He told himself, not for the first time, that there was
no reason he had to like this man.

"This is more than a joke. Or it will be. You'll understand that soon." Buren drew on his cigarette until it flared and died. He flicked the butt into the mud for the investigation of the magpies. "They've apparently discovered a most insidious pleasure," he continued. "I wouldn't have thought it of C.D., but Charlotte sounded like she was being fucked by a bull."

"Shut up, Buren."

"That is a typically inadequate response. Just what I'd expect from you."

"Shut up."

"You really didn't know, did you?" Buren clapped his hands together in silent applause. "You pay so much attention to this sinkhole ranch you don't even recognize the true threats to it."

"I'm not interested in your predictions of disaster," he said, gathering himself. "You need to haul that load of poison back with you to Cheyenne. C.D. and Charlotte can take care of themselves."

"They'll take care of themselves and more," Buren said, amused. "You'll be picking up the pieces until Christmas."

He hadn't known. Or had he? Charlotte and Hobbs each tended to their own chores on the ranch, working in the meshed silence he preferred. It was true they'd both begun coming to him with new ideas, small ideas, about how he might change something with the horses or feed storage or the furnace in the house. They gave off prospects for change like sparks. But they never came to him together. They avoided each other when he was around. He had noticed that. He'd just misconstrued the reasons why.

He tried to work some feeling into his suddenly numb fingers. All right. It was a fact. Charlotte had seduced Hobbs. Although he didn't like to consider the details, it was hard to see the problem there except for the inevitable one of how Hobbs would handle things when Charlotte decided to leave. She would never settle down on the Trumpet Bell. Buren was wrong to think so.

Buren left for Cheyenne without another word, and the afternoon filled itself with a host of remembered sighs and glances. Once Adams admitted the truth of the situation, he couldn't get the evidence out of his mind. He recalled how he'd helped Hobbs Sheetrock the tiny room at the back of the machine shed that had been framed out for the storage of bottled sheep dips. Hobbs hadn't slept in the house since Charlotte's arrival, a choice that seemed practical at the time. He'd swept out the shed room, gotten himself a mattress from a church sale and said nothing about comfort or discomfort. The dogs slept with Hobbs on most nights; that was all Adams knew. Now, he couldn't get the image of his sister washing the breakfast dishes, her shirt covered with black and white collie hair, out of his roiling head. God damn attention-getting Charlotte. He needed to have a serious talk with his sister.

He found Charlotte in the barn, putting a halter on the plate-footed buckskin gelding that supposedly belonged to him although he hadn't ridden the animal since Charlotte had come back home. His sister looked contained and ordinary, if her kind of stubborn beauty could ever be called ordinary. Her face was flushed. Her light blue eyes were wholly focused on the buckskin because she needed his attention. She was gentle in her movements, offhandedly graceful. But he still couldn't picture her as Hobbs's full-fledged lover. Jesus. What a turn. His sister was sleeping with his misfit friend. The thought should have filled him with sly laughter, but it didn't.

"Buren is one big black cloud. I don't know why he bothered to come out here." Charlotte winked at him after she buckled the halter on the horse.

"I'm sure he wouldn't say it was family duty."

"I'm sure he wouldn't," she said. "You're the only one of us afflicted with that."

It wasn't what he had expected her to say. He waited to see if she would push at him again.

"You know what I want, Fremont? Really?"

He had no idea, but he opened the stall door for her so she could bring out the buckskin. When she was absolutely young, Charlotte had wanted everything.

"Privacy?" It was a word that took a lot for him to say.

"You shit." Charlotte burst into a loud, happy laugh, one that showed her teeth. She led the gelding past him, still laughing, and he smelled the slight sweetness of her washed hair as it mixed with horse dander and sweat. "Buren tattled on me, didn't he? He was always like that, taking secrets to people he thought were in charge. No wonder he works for the governor. He's a snake. You're not a snake."

"It's probably not my business, whatever you're doing."

"No, it's not. But it might take you awhile to get used to that fact. Leave it alone, okay?"

He started to agree that he would leave it alone, but a persistent vision of Hobbs—shivering in shock and pain—stopped him. It had been a long, long time since he'd left Hobbs purely alone. There were obligations. He'd never been able to quite explain them, even to himself, but they were there.

Charlotte glanced at him, her face proud with affection. She held out a striped saddle blanket, and he could see the sore, bitten nails of her hand. "That's not the favor I'm asking for, Fremont. You'll have to trust C.D. and me. What I really want is for you to ride up the butte with me. Let's take some time off. Let's go see the petroglyphs and those caves where we used to hunt for bobcat. They're still there, aren't they? They haven't disappeared? I'd like to spend some time poking around in the old places. It brings back good memories of when Ma and Dad were alive." She paused to slip the blanket across the buckskin's bony withers. "Don't make fun of the idea, either. And don't pretend your frozen-off toes make it hard to keep your feet in the stirrups. That's a fake excuse. You're not as old and washed up as you want to pretend. Neither of you are. Just come with me for a little while. That's all you've got to do."

And he believed her because he wanted to.

While their mother was still alive, Adams had felt nothing but protective of Charlotte. He would have said that he stood on one side of Charlotte and their mother stood on the other side, and together they were like hardwood shims driven into the earth to brace a leaning pole. After their mother died, Charlotte wasn't exactly helpless. That would never be the case. But Adams managed to lose his way with his sister for several years.

Portia Laury Adams's death in 1961 was unexpected, but not tragic, and its aftermath was all that she would have hoped for: tidy and well-spoken. Buren was in Denver in those days, married to a tall, narrow-shouldered woman who worked in a bank. Charlotte was finishing her degree at the university in Laramie. Uncle Gene Laury had taken the train from Rawlins to Salt Lake to conduct business there, so Adams was left on the ranch with his mother; C.D. Hobbs, who was an excellent hand when the voices were quiet in his head; and the brothers Steve and Nod Barnheisel. It was lambing season. The nights were dry, but cold enough to make their white breath sink below their faces as they moved back and forth under the black canopy of the sky. Adams alternated birthing shifts with Hobbs, whom he trusted with the animals. Each of them had a Barnheisel for help, although Nod Barnheisel had to be watched because he sometimes got sloppy despite his extensive knowledge of sheep.

Hobbs woke Adams from the inadequate tumble of a single hour's sleep. A young ewe was in a bad way. Adams followed Hobbs downstairs where he stepped into his waiting coveralls and knotted the caked laces of his boots. He tried to ready himself. He knew the ewe's dumb, visible pain was about to replace the weak grasp of his dreams. Hobbs turned up the light of the lantern he carried, and they made the piercing, gratifying walk to the sheds together. Adams couldn't help but feel pride when he looked at the low, clean shapes of the lambing sheds. The Trumpet Bell was going forward: new grazing leases, new loans, the shrewd sale of feeder lambs, rail cars lashed with bales of high-grade wool. He and his uncle and the diplomacy of his mother had made it so. He didn't want to lose the ewe in her first labor, but if he did lose her, he would go past her loss and the loss of others. There was satisfaction out there somewhere, knowledge of a job well done. The war in Korea had changed him as much as it had changed C.D. Hobbs. A sheep man's satisfaction—limited, achievable—was the only satisfaction he now cared to pursue.

The ewe was too small, so he crossed the frozen mud of the ranch yard toward the house where he removed his boots before climbing the stairs to wake his mother. She was sixty-two years old. She prepared herself carefully, but quickly, then walked with Adams to the milk and blood heat of the sheds. They didn't speak. The ewe was down, exhausted by hours of contractions. The bulging glaze of her upturned eye told them they had little time before they would have to take the lamb by knife and leave the mother to bleed out.

Portia Adams whispered to the animal as she knelt beside it, her blessedly small-boned hands encased in the sterile gloves Hobbs had prepared for her. She slid a hand past the ewe's swollen vulva and worked her slim fingers to straighten the bent knees of the unborn lamb. She maneuvered for a hard moment to bring the tiny, pliant hooves into the birth canal and in line with the lamb's tapered jaw. The wiry muscles of her bare forearm clenched beneath her pale, age-slackened skin as the ewe's insides clenched, and both of them trembled together in silence. Hobbs stayed at the ewe's head to keep her from bolting from the pain. Adams bent near his mother and tried not to fret about a prolapsed uterus and infection and every other disaster he could predict.

When Portia Adams was sure of the lamb's position, she withdrew her slick, steaming arm and looked at her numbed fingers with something like surprise. She'd done it many times, but helping with a birth remained remarkable even to her. She told Adams she didn't think the ewe was carrying twins. "There's just the one, and it's alive," she said. "We can hope for the best."

There wasn't much fresh blood. With Hobbs at her head, the ewe found her strength and delivered the lamb, but Portia Adams didn't stay to see the gangly buck gain his feet. She prized the sleep she found so easily in winter when the sky was like a swift, dark sail. She left the shed as quietly as she

had arrived. When Adams went back into the house, bootless
again and tired from a thousand familiar worries, he found his
mother dead in the upstairs bedroom she'd shared with his father, a pair of undyed wool blankets pulled above her deflated
chest. Her white hair was loose across the pillow. It still held
the scalloped waves of its braids and pins. He had come to
thank her. On his way into the house, he'd re-hung the large
coat she'd worn to the sheds—it was one of Gene's. He would
forever remember how well it smelled of cold air and straw.

He waited with her awhile. He was better at sensing last
chances now that he was older and had seen men fight each
other and die, and he took the opportunity to be alone with his
mother perhaps because they had been alone together so little.
He loved her. He knew that. And she'd known it. The love had
never been a secret feeling.

He remembered her visit to the naval hospital in California,
his last stop before his discharge from the marines. "We know
we're blessed to have you back, son," she said. "I can't tell you
how blessed I feel. Other families—" She bowed her head.
"You'll do fine, you know, even without those toes. You'll adjust. Things won't be the same, but they'll be worth every bit
of heart you've got left." He didn't share with her the details
of what had happened in Korea. He hoarded every uncertain
feeling he had about what he had seen and done at Chosin.
His mother, however, talked to him about Hobbs—the way
C.D. had been with Adams and gotten so terribly burned and
how Adams might start to feel guilty about that. His mother's
straightforward questions and answers led him back toward a
life he actually imagined he might lead. She retrieved him from
the prison of his doubts. Now he would stay by her bedside as
she had stayed by his.

When the dawn was no longer indeterminate and gray, he
telephoned Buren in Denver. Then he called his uncle's hotel
in Salt Lake. He dreaded breaking the news to Charlotte and
Hobbs. His sister, he decided, deserved better than a phone
call. He would drive the 150 miles to Laramie and tell her they

had lost their mother. Hobbs—who was owed a nearly equal gesture—would get the most Adams could summon at that moment. For he was feeling it now, the weight of his middle age and the flailing grief of a child all at once. His eyes were thick and hot with tears. He would miss her more than he'd missed anything in his life.

Hobbs was still in the sheds with Steve and Nod and the neighbor, Bud Rorty, who had arrived to help out during the day. The night crew had overseen the delivery of thirty-eight lambs with only one stillbirth. It had been a good shift. Adams didn't give himself time to plan his announcement. He was afraid he'd break down. "C.D.," he said, rasping into the impossible sentence. "C.D., my ma has died."

Hobbs's dirty face went raw-colored above the immediate spasms of its muscles. He began to weep. He didn't ask details or questions. He just stepped into the straw-bale enclosure he'd built for the orphaned lambs, and he crouched under the bright heat lamp he'd set up to warm the orphans, and he wept some more. Bud Rorty hung his head alongside the hung heads of the Barnheisels, all of them stained from foot to brow with blood and strands of mucus and liquid shit. Bud stuttered out an offer. "I c...can call my brother, Tom. For extra help," he said. "Y..you know I'm sorry, Fremont. She was always good to me." Adams nodded. They would need help from people like the Rortys and the Gundersons because the new lambs would keep coming hour after hour, day after day, even though he needed to bury his mother.

Before he left to change clothes for the hard drive to Laramie, Adams went to Hobbs by the straw bales and reached for his shoulder with both hands. It was the unburned shoulder, round and strong. He waited for Hobbs to lift his face, then he asked Hobbs to look after things and to be with the doctor when the doctor got there. "Sit with her," he said, his words as light as powdered chalk. "In that rocking chair up there. She'd like that." Then he walked away from the sheds, dazed by the cries of his hundreds and hundreds of sheep as those cries rose into the unpainted dome of morning. The sound was as constant and unsorted as it had always been, but he heard it differently now—the pitched noise of birth and its many hungers.

He rode with Charlotte through the narrow arm of alfalfa their mother had called Creek Meadow with Charlotte opening and closing both gates from atop the buckskin, working the horse backward and forward with careful pressure from one leg and then the other. He rode the old bay horse, Redrock, at his sister's request. They went uphill toward the iron-fenced graveyard that held their parents and Uncle Gene and Blue Pete Tosh, who had died of a stroke when they were children. Blue Pete's funeral—a short prayer and one old Scots hymn sung without accompaniment—was the first funeral they'd ever attended. Since her arrival, Charlotte kept glass jars filled with aster and yarrow and shooting star on their parents' sunken graves. The graveyard thrummed with the sound of slow, heavy bees at work on the blossoms.

"There's a hummingbird that comes up here in the evenings," she said. "I can't imagine where it nests. The ranch looks like nothing but rock and sand."

"We could use more rain," he said, dismounting.

"Gene's grave doesn't get any flowers from me." Charlotte had both hands on her hips, opinionated. "You were always his favorite. Maybe you can design him a monument of sheep dung."

"He'd like that, and you know it," Adams said, thinking of his uncle's painful struggle with mouth cancer. "It would make him proud."

"If he was still alive—or if Ma hadn't died so young—you'd be playing second fiddle around here. You ever think of that?" Charlotte plucked some wilted flowers from the jar on their mother's grave and tossed them into the shearing currents of a breeze.

"No." Gene Laury had died in 1965, the prime sheep man of the family, and the one who'd really nailed the Adams family to the huge, dry parchment of the land.

"You aren't very curious about what might happen, are you, Fremont? You don't speculate."

"I guess not. I try to be practical."

"And successful?"

"You think so?" His heart skipped a partial beat as he asked his question. He wanted his sister to admire him.

"By Uncle Gene's rawhide standards, you are a success. Hell, yes."

They remounted, and Charlotte let the buckskin pick its way toward the two-track that led up and around Bell Butte. Adams relaxed into the cantle of his saddle and allowed Redrock to follow on loose rein. The graveyard's iron fence needed a fresh coat of paint, but the view was good from there. He liked how the long, sallow curve of Powder Rim mended itself to the cobalt sky that lorded it over the distant southern mountains. Bell Butte also threw a shirttail of cool shadow over the graveyard at this hour, as it did on most mornings. Uncle Gene had said he would always appreciate that shade.

His mind drifted to memories of his mother's burial. The service had been simple. Buren and his wife were more hesitant than they'd ever been about family matters, which made Adams grateful. Charlotte was wrung and knotted with grief. She would only go as far as the corral to look at her horse with his rough, ungroomed winter coat before she returned to the house and their mother's room upstairs. Uncle Gene Laury appeared disoriented, unsure of every habit he'd ever had because he had somehow outlived his sister and her husband and was left to shelter himself on land that had become mostly theirs. It helped to know that the passing had been peaceful. Portia's many friends said it was what she would have wanted. And while Adams knew those friends were right because he had seen the contours of a lasting sleep on his mother's face, sentiments of that sort contorted his sister with anger.

"She should have been seeing a doctor," Charlotte screeched, lashing out at Adams. "She shouldn't have been working so hard. *You* let her work too hard."

Adams didn't feel the emptiness that way. He and Gene and

C.D. Hobbs finished with the lambs because they had to. It was good for them, Adams thought, that the work didn't stop. His mother had understood that. She had always stood by the dragline of ranch work. His mother would have emphasized the good fruits of their labors: the healthy Corriedale-Rambouillet crossbreds, the plentiful forage, the champion bucks that would bring high prices at the Casper sales. She would not have wanted her death to be any kind of interruption.

But it was. Portia Adams's death changed so much. Neither Charlotte nor Buren returned to the Trumpet Bell, except for the most cursory holiday visits. Even Hobbs used the occasion to initiate another departure. He and Adams were hanging a new corral gate a few days after the funeral when Hobbs announced he was leaving for a construction job he'd heard about in Nevada.

"You're taking off?" Adams had considered the possibility that his mother's death might lever things upside down for Hobbs—might even lead to a bad spell and new doses of calming medications—but he hadn't expected the man to run away. He had somehow thought they'd work it out together, what it meant to be part of a small and shrinking family.

"Mine's down in Trinidad, last I heard," Hobbs said, speaking of his own mother. "Living with a miner's got disability."

This wasn't news to Adams. He'd heard it many times.

"Your mother was the best teacher Dixon school ever had. She was a good person, and she was nice to me, and careful in her planning. You're like her, Fremont, in more ways than the shape of your face."

Adams felt a wrenching in his bowels just behind his belt buckle. They had been through this at the funeral and the wake, all of it. He really didn't want to wrestle with the spilling sweats of his grief yet again. He tried to focus on the fat hinges of the corral gate.

"You ever think of getting married? Because I remember how your mother used to—"

"Shut it, C.D." Adams did not want to betray how much

the question surprised him. He kept his eyes on the gatepost and concentrated on the strong smells of wood and rust.

"It's a lot to think about, I know. Nod says—"

"Nod doesn't know shit. You'll become a permanent idiot if you listen to Nod. Be better off in Nevada." He could hear Hobbs working his heels down into his boots. "I'm not gonna talk about getting married just because she's gone. That's what those words are for, you know it too, so don't bring it up again. It hasn't even been a week. Right now, everything I work on— the herd, the house, money, furniture, food—is all about my mother being gone. I got Charlotte to think of."

It was Hobbs's turn to be caught off guard. Adams watched his face go tight across the cheeks. "Charlotte." He gave the name its own kind of unscaled melody.

"Yeah, my sister. Remember her? She graduates from college in a couple of months. This has been tough on her. She might need some time."

"Time for what?"

"To act like a kid. Or not. To decide to live here after graduation—which I'm praying she won't do. To get over what's happened and leave me with the bills and the ghosts. She's taking it hard. You've seen that."

"So are you." Hobbs held up his left hand to placate Adams. All five of his fingers were trembling. "You're taking it real hard."

"Yeah . . . but. . . ." Adams swallowed. "Yes. I am. But there's less of me left to bring down in a sad time. You know that better than anybody, C.D. I've lost trust in a lot of things. Ma understood that, and she understood I did fine if I stayed close to home. But if Nevada works for you, go to Nevada. I guess I'm glad you got the spirit to give it a try."

He didn't see Hobbs again for many, many years.

When they left the two-track to ride under Chin Rock, Charlotte let Adams take the lead. He wanted to stop and add a stone to Old Etchepare's cairn. Charlotte was whistling now, and there was a chickadee whistling out on the prairie, and there were moments when Adams couldn't tell the two songs apart. He got off Redrock at the cairn, his saddle creaking under the shift of his weight, and he draped the horse's reins over a tall, silvered grapple of sage. Old Etch hadn't wanted to be buried in the family plot or in the cemetery of the Catholic church in Rawlins, which was where most dead sheepherders ended up. He wanted to rest above his favorite winter bedding ground, just where he'd parked the sheep wagon year after year, in the lee of the smooth jut of sandstone that resembled a determined human chin. Old Etch had asked for a cairn to mark the spot—nothing more—and after nearly twenty years the cairn was thick and wide and as well-fitted as a homesteader's wall. Adams searched the ground for a small piece of gun-black chert he could slip into an empty crack. Just a token.

"He never wanted to leave here," Adams said, mounting up again and resetting his straw hat against the freshening breeze. "Not for Spain or California or anywhere else he ever talked about. Ma always wondered what happened to his money."

"The usual, don't you think—women, drink, gambling," said Charlotte. "Though I wanted to believe he sent it to a true love in Basque country, like she was his waiting princess."

"He was the only person I ever knew besides Dad who joked about what people were trying to do out here. He said most of our land was good for nothing *but* sheep, which was nice because no other fools would ever want to take it from us. He was right about that." Adams paused to wet his mouth with spit. "Remember how he used to sing? He'd sing day and night when he was herding in the basin. Said there were godless places in the world meant for nothing but the wind and the basin was one of them. Said you had to protect yourself by singing on ground like that. You couldn't trust it because it didn't feature snakes or saints."

Charlotte grinned, her corn-silk hair blowing loose from its braids and whipping across her mouth. "It's a wonder we're not more superstitious than we are, growing up around Etch and Basilio and Blue Pete."

"Maybe we should be," he said, thinking of his years of Korean nightmares, their chaos and cold.

"No. Those men were better than any church when it came to spinning out beliefs. They had it all woven together like a rug. But we're not like that. At least I'm not, though it's no fault of San Francisco's that I don't believe in much. That's a city full of lit candles."

"The noise of a big city would get to me," he said.

"No, it wouldn't. It's the options that would drive you crazy, Fremont. The way a person can choose who she wants to be. You actually like your lack of choices."

"Maybe so."

"There's no maybe about it. You've got more crust than a loaf of petrified bread."

Adams paused, trying to decide whether Charlotte really wanted to quarrel with him. Certain things—certain placid responsibilities—*were* easy for him. He had only to look at Buren and Charlotte across the vast gulfs of their differences to see that. He was made to be predictable, to see the advantages of a rigorous, marginal life. He was made to breed animals that thrived on lousy grass and to cajole trickles of water into dusty fields. Agricultural failure didn't faze him much. Bad weather and bad luck with livestock wasn't something a man should take personally. But Charlotte and Buren—they took the episodes of the Trumpet Bell very personally. Buren said he looked forward to the day when the three of them would agree to sell the whole damn opera. Charlotte, whom they rarely saw and almost never heard from, was the opposite. She wanted the Trumpet Bell to remain in the family, but it was to remain as she chose to remember it: vital, comic, independent, and enviable. Their home place was the permanent shelter for her ideals, no matter how far from those ideals she traveled.

Charlotte's voice intruded on his scattered thoughts. "What?" he said, giving her his attention. "Did you want to pick on me again?"

Charlotte leaned back in her saddle. "I asked if you ever thought about getting married."

"Oh, damn. Here we go."

"I sort of liked that Patterson girl from town. What was her name?"

"Julie. And you sure didn't seem to like her at the time."

"Well, maybe I wasn't so *neutral* back then. Maybe I thought you were trying to replace Ma with a teenage tramp."

He thought about Julie Patterson, how he'd hauled her off to elk camps and hunters' motels just to find some relief. She would have married him if he'd had the decency to ask. Her father, who knew Adams's motives better than he knew them himself, finally sent Julie to live with a cousin in Rapid City. "Hobbs got married once." He raised his voice to cover the distance between them. "About three weeks after our mother's funeral."

"You're kidding." Charlotte reined the buckskin to a quick halt. "You're just saying that to change the subject."

Adams kept his head low so Charlotte couldn't see his bitter grin. "He hasn't told you about it, has he? It was a neighbor of his aunt's down in Craig, what you *could* call a tramp. She smoked and drank C.D.'s wages, then asked for a divorce after he found her on top of her real boyfriend."

"Don't be rude."

"I'm sorry." He nudged Redrock ahead of the stalled buckskin on the narrow trail. "Well, maybe I'm not really sorry. Maybe I do have a point. You need to know that Hobbs sometimes . . . well, he reacts in big ways when he gets emotional. He doesn't have a regular governor on him like most of us. He don't talk about what he'll do, he just does it."

"And you think I need to be warned about that? You think being emotional is bad?" Exasperation crackled into Charlotte's voice.

"I don't know what I think. Maybe you don't either. Which is probably why we're both out here."

They rode in silence for several long minutes. The terrain became steeper, threaded with winding game trails, pocked by the burrows of nocturnal animals. Adams took note of the fresh scraps of fur and skin that were all that remained of an unlucky rabbit. Owl, he thought. The owls had always hunted hard through here.

Charlotte broke the moody quiet. "You ever consider how easy things would have been for us if Dad had stayed alive?" It was a pinprick of a question for her to ask, and she knew it. She rode right up on Redrock's flank in order to catch Adams's eye. Her lips looked flaky and pale. "He would have found more money. He would have made better choices than Gene. He always did." Charlotte had been very young—no more than twelve—when David Keith MacGregor Adams was killed. She had always carried a torch for his memory, and she had never tolerated criticism of his faults or eccentric behaviors. But David Adams had been killed—or had pretty much killed himself, as Buren put it—when he was blown off a wellhead being set by a feckless neighbor. The death had brought the family something the Trumpet Bell sorely needed at the time: an infusion of cash.

"He did have his resources," Adams said, smiling at a memory of his father in a dapper houndstooth suit. David Adams had stepped off the train at Fort Steele in 1920 with nothing more than a cardboard suitcase and a good head for numbers. A few years later he married the Dixon schoolteacher, Portia Laury, and began buying tracts of abandoned land with her brother Gene. David Adams should not have been much of a rancher. There wasn't anything ruthless or wind-burned about him. He merely acquired mortgages and paid them off. Yet that, and a sky-high tolerance for unforgiving weather, was really all it took.

"He would have taken care of us," Charlotte said, fiercely. "You know Ma believed that." Adams reckoned that their mother had believed in nothing more than their father's gregariousness. It was David Adams's enthusiasm that caused him to stop when he saw Sock Jarvis on that fresh well pad with a roustabout crew. Nobody who knew David Adams had ever seen him turn away in the face of another's need. He had removed his jacket and climbed the derrick with a wrench stuck deep in his waistband. Sock Jarvis was sheltered by the flatbed of a truck when it happened. He lived through the blast, losing David Adams and two Texans he'd hired in a Rawlins bar. Sock Jarvis visited with Portia Adams after the funeral and put her in touch with a Denver banker, but Portia Adams never told anybody the details of what Jarvis said to her, how he had tried to put things right.

"Ma believed a lot of things," he said, steering Redrock across a gully along the neckline of Bell Butte. "She was good that way."

"And neither of us has that capacity? Is that what you're suggesting?"

"I'm not suggesting anything, Charlotte. You just got done telling me how I'm not ever curious. And you remember Dad different than I do. That's your right. I like how you see us all in your own particular way. I'm just saying neither of us is exactly like our mother. We're different, times are different. That's just how it works."

"Well, I am." His sister turned again in her saddle. Her squinting eyes were fractured with a clear, insistent light. "I am more like her than you or Buren or anybody else. Portia Adams was a female ass kicker, way before her time. She had guts and smarts and loyalty. You aren't going to deny that."

He wasn't. He also wasn't going to suggest that Portia Adams would never have done something as manipulative and self-serving as making love to C.D. Hobbs.

When they got to the dead juniper tree that marked the farthest point the horses could climb, Adams told Charlotte to go on ahead. He didn't feel the need to scramble to the top of Bell Butte. He said, "I think I'm in the right frame of mind to enjoy this tree and its shade." Charlotte didn't hesitate. She was energized by his weakness or laziness, whichever it was, and she headed up the boulder-strewn trail alone, at a run. "Ass kicker," she shouted as she sped around a switchback thirty feet above him. "I kick. You lose."

She was still agile enough to negotiate the tricky, peeling rock of the butte's single spire. Before long, he saw her far above him, searching for old handholds and footholds as she climbed higher and higher. As she grappled her way across the wide, copper-colored rib lines of stone, she gestured at him with the occasional free hand, laughing, probably taunting. Her face was white and bud-shaped in the glare of the sun. She looked like a clinging spar of bone to him, like a reed of impetuousness and cloth. Charlotte Adams. She was back. She was happy. She wanted to frolic on the ranch with her brother, and she wanted to remake both the ranch and brother in her own image. It was a recipe for disaster. He knew that now. He removed the saddles from both horses, pleased to engage in a task he could actually manage. The two geldings hung their heads and quietly fought the flies with patient switches of their tails. What the hell was he going to do with his livewire sister? This was the question he was forced to ask himself. And what the hell was she going to do to him and C.D. Hobbs?

Hobbs and Charlotte allowed what was between them to grow and test itself against every hard surface they could find. Charlotte came for Hobbs in the middle of the day and took him upstairs into the room that had been hers since birth, leading him away from the workbench or the fence line or the seat of Adams's truck. He went shyly, at first, but always without resistance. Charlotte made love to him—Adams didn't care to know the details—then sent him back to his tasks. She sometimes walked with him into the ranch yard wearing nothing more than panties and an unbuttoned shirt. She would hang on him a little at those moments, filching reluctant kisses from his lips, though this only occurred when Maria Delores was safely out of sight.

They spent their nights in the machine shed. At first, there wasn't any drinking, at least not during the day, and the worst Adams could make of the situation was the inconvenience of losing Hobbs's help for an hour, though Hobbs was always good for any job once he got back to it. But Charlotte wasn't interested in arrangements or limits. She and Hobbs began to stay in the house, heaving and moaning into the night, bathing in the one tub together at unpredictable times, staggering to breakfast in a parade of bare haunches and yawns. Adams knew Charlotte was just waiting, waiting, waiting for him to complain, so he didn't. It would all spill over soon—the extra feeling would spill over—he kept telling himself that. There would be equilibrium. What he was dealing with was a temporary human intoxication.

But some nights the coils of wet towel on the bathroom floor and the smell of riven woman drove him toward Baggs and the trailer home of a woman who charged him a few dollars for her time. She had two young children, and Adams was shocked by the constancy of his lust in the face of their simple entreaties and the inane sounds of the television shows that leaked through every wall of the trailer. He hadn't been so filled with need since he was a nineteen-year-old marine waiting for combat assignment in Japan. He began to wonder what unseen carcass they were all feeding on.

"She will suck him dry," Buren said. Buren relished his weekly phone calls from Cheyenne. They allowed him to castigate his younger brother from a comfortable distance. "She will suck him dry every way you can imagine because she is easily bored and can't help herself. And she'll suck you dry, too, because that's what she's really after."

"It's not like that," Adams said. He tried to talk about how good Hobbs looked and how much work they were getting done together. He did not mention that he felt pushed out of his own house.

"You wait," Buren said. "The next grand item on the agenda will be a baby or money. Mark my words. When you hear those sweet notes, my brother, you will realize which piper is calling the tune."

Then Charlotte brought drink into it, though he would never know why. Bottles of fruit wine were opened at dinner, before dinner, and after dinner when they all smoked their silent cigarettes. Bottles of vodka appeared to celebrate meteor showers or the birth of Nan's pups. Omero, in his most solicitous way, asked Adams if he would need his help after the end of October. This was how he let Adams know he and Maria

Delores were prepared to leave their jobs. Adams asked Omero to stay on, but he continued to drink vodka with Hobbs and Charlotte, and sometimes without them, because he didn't care for the sweetness of fruit wine. He kept a separate bottle for his drives to the woman he paid for sex, emptying the bottle with her while they were naked in the bedroom that was only large enough for a bed. He smashed the bottles on the road as he drove back to the ranch, hurling them into the black nothingness torn open by the roar of his truck.

One evening, Hobbs didn't come to the house for dinner. Adams ate his antelope sausage and rice in silence, waiting for an explanation from Charlotte that never came. He washed and dried the dishes before his impatience got the best of him.

"Is your friend sleeping one off?" he asked.

"No. C.D.'s sick, since you're asking. His head aches. He said he might not be able to ride the ditches tomorrow morning."

The two of them were on the porch, looking into the rough glitter of the night. Charlotte poured him a jelly glass of apple wine, and he took it. Her hair was down, mussed and uncombed. Her lips were so dark with color they looked like glazed shadows. He wanted her to say more because as far as he knew Hobbs had never been physically too sick to work a day in his life.

"He'll be fine," she continued. "I think he's just tired."

"Maybe you could give him a break. He is forty-four years old." He tried to make the suggestion without malice.

"That doesn't seem to stop you any." She giggled, and he wondered what, if anything, he could hide from Charlotte. All of them—brothers and sister—had the awful gift of seeing right through one another. She'd been visiting friends and neighbors, and had somehow found out about the woman in Baggs. She'd no doubt also heard plenty of talk about the other places his dick had been over the last fifteen years.

"We're not talking about me. I still get to work in the morning."

"He wants to try for a baby."

When he heard those words his fingers went as cold as the

captured light of the stars above them. He tried not to let
Buren's acid voice into his head, but it was there anyway, telling him to bolt the gates and bar the doors. "Are you saying
you want a baby?"

She shrugged. It was a loose-jointed, wanton gesture meant
to gouge him. "No, C.D. wants one. I'm just going along with
the world."

Adams shook his head, trying to clear it. "You've never gone
along with anything for the hell of it. That's not your style. I'm
sorry things didn't work out with Elon the way you wanted,
but you shouldn't play helpless with Hobbs."

Another giggle. It was hard to tell how much wine was in
her talk. "Take it easy, Fremont. Go with the flow. I give him
something. He gives me something. We aren't signing on some
permanent dotted line."

"How about C.D. gives you something and you take it? You
didn't see him when he showed up here this spring, Charlotte.
I did. I don't know where he'd been, or what was chasing him,
but he was in bad shape. He looked like a lamb with scabies.
He couldn't talk with regular sentences. He's not a regular person. You need to go easy on him."

"No, I don't. That's your bullshit, your guilt bullshit you
never cleaned up. You think he's as fragile as a butterfly." She
wasn't shouting, but her voice was high, and it worked its way
into his ears like a barbed instrument. "He told me what happened in Korea. Everything you never talk about. Everything
bad. I *know,* okay? So don't get all high and mighty with me."

The shame that was always in him rose and ate at his
tongue, but he fought it down and swallowed its biting juices.
Charlotte couldn't know what had happened at Chosin because
Hobbs couldn't remember it. She was guessing. Prodding at
him like he was a caged bear. "You shouldn't talk about what
you don't understand," he said. "C.D. and me *understand* each
other and how certain things have to be left alone. We don't
go digging inside each other for everything that's there. So I'm
telling—not asking—I'm telling you not to dig inside his head.

Hump him all you want. Tie an apron on and have his baby. Put up a life on this ranch. There will always be a place for you here." He heard her breathing get short. He'd called her bluff, and the comment about the apron had made her mad. "But you need to stop with your failed ambitions and whatnot," he continued. "Don't bring that California garbage out here. Don't dump that stuff on a simple man like C.D. Hobbs."

"Simple? When I tell him you—"

"He won't do a thing. He knows exactly who he is, unlike the rest of us. And I know he's better than us both."

She threw the wine bottle first. It hit him in the chest with no real force, but her glass caught him on the cheekbone and cut him and irrigated his eye with the burn of cheap alcohol. She was gone, off the porch in a dervish of hair and skirts, before he could wipe his face clean. He watched her flee to the small room in the back of the machine shed where Hobbs was apparently resting. Despite how good it felt, he knew he'd been stupid. It was never smart to go to war against somebody like Charlotte. But she'd given him the opportunity, and he'd reached right for it.

What he didn't expect: the way Charlotte went to battle with no rules and no dignity except the perceived dignity of her own opinions. Because he did bear a heavy burden of shame about the past, and she sensed it, and she was shameless. She dispatched Hobbs to plead with him. And Hobbs didn't even know what his role in the dispute was. He and Adams hadn't talked about Charlotte, not since she'd shown up and replaced all the kid stories they told about her with her real self. They took refuge in what was always the same about each other— the agreed-upon silences, the routine humor, the words and tools that solved familiar problems of water and soil. There had never been a morning in their whole lives when they couldn't meet up in the barn or the kitchen and hit their stride together. Now Hobbs wanted to talk to him about engagement rings.

"It might be early, I know she hadn't been here—"

"You want to marry Charlotte? Did she tell you to say that?" Adams was so shocked his choked-off words sounded firm and steady.

"I hadn't asked her yet." Hobbs ducked his head into the tight cotton collar of his shirt. They were standing in the truck bed and cleaning one of the silos for a delivery of seed cake. Both of them were covered in the beige grit of leftover feed. "I'm asking what you think I ought to do."

"Is she pregnant?"

Hobbs swatted his wrench against a rusty leg of the silo. "God damn it, Fremont, don't . . . don't get nasty about your own sister. I feel bad enough. It ain't right, how we've done things. Your mother would've killed me and run me off if—"

"Ma died when Charlotte was twenty-one. I would've killed you if you'd touched her then." He kept an unmoving stare on Hobbs.

Hobbs ducked his head again. "There's no baby yet, but Charlotte wants one. I hope you know how I feel about her. I feel like it's all worth it. Every day of my life—even the bad ones—has been worth it to get to this point. I've known her forever. We can do all right together. We've talked about it enough."

The hope in his eyes was fresh and killing. He believed in all of it—the love, the drowsy, paired talk, the perfection of family. Hobbs had pure faith, and he, Adams, no longer had any capacity for that word. And that's what Hobbs really wanted from him, wasn't it? His faith. The diamond ring was just a pretense.

"Listen to me, C.D. You're the best man I know."

"You wouldn't say that if you'd seen—"

"Be quiet, damn it. Hear me out." And he banged his own crescent wrench against the silo until it rang out like a giant bell. "I'm gonna say what I'm gonna say. You can be with Charlotte. You can do what you want, get married, settle down, and I won't stand in your way. But you got to let me say a few things about my crazy god damn sister. She's been talking plenty about me."

Hobbs pawed at the mismatched skin of his neck, then covered it with a rumpled glove. His breathing was quick and shallow as if he was trying not to cry. "It's not like that," he said. "I wouldn't let nothing I do get between you and Charlotte."

"It *is* like that," Adams said, leaning into his vehemence, "but it's not your fault or mine. You remember that. Charlotte wants to rule the roost. She likes to be the boss, and that means taking me down a notch or two. She wants to run things. I want to make sure you understand what's going on. Do you? Can we agree on that much right now?"

But Hobbs agreed to nothing. In fact, he stopped talking altogether, and when they finished their work at the silo, he signed to Adams that he'd rather walk back to the house with the collie, Sol, than share a ride in the truck. That suited Adams just fine. Watching Hobbs under the feeble autumn sun, seeing him hitch at the loose waist of his jeans made Adams want to hit something. He wanted to throw a punch. Tear something apart. How had he let himself be played for such an idiot? Why couldn't his sister keep her god damn selfishness to her self?

Charlotte confronted him before he got inside the house. She seemed to have guessed what had happened at the silo, and she trembled with anger, her eyes violet and damp with the temper she never revealed to Hobbs. "You told him to end it, didn't you?" she shouted. "You told him to dump me without knowing it wouldn't work."

Adams found himself watching the full maneuver of her lips. "He asked me about engagement rings."

She went on as if she hadn't heard him. "It's because you think he isn't grateful. You think he should be grateful and bow down in front of you every day because of everything you've done for him, and now he doesn't do that."

"I don't think anybody should bow down to anybody else, Charlotte. C.D. needs to make sure he takes care of himself. I'm trying to do that. Some things are too much for him to handle."

"No, *we're* too much for you to handle. That's the real problem."

"Maybe. That could be part of what's under my skin. I'm sure you'd like me out of the mix so you can speed on through your love."

She was in jeans and wool socks with a new chambray shirt she'd bought for Hobbs knotted around her waist. Her hair was up in red-gold braids, which meant she planned to take one of the horses out for a ride. "I still own a third of this ranch, Fremont. C.D. and I can take it away from you whenever we want."

"I don't think so. You'd need Buren's help to do that, and Buren is rarely inclined to help anybody. Besides, none of this is about taking anything away from me. Not if you really think about it." He felt a blatant calm begin to take root in his body. It warmed him from head to heel. "Did C.D. really talk about Korea? Did he tell you about going cuckoo over there?"

His words froze her solid, just as he'd thought they would. His sister, he told himself, was a storm to be weathered. Outlasting her would take only resolve and a willingness to be battered.

"You were too young to know how bad the fighting was. He probably saved my life—that's true. I'll never forget it. But he wasn't much better than a slobbering baby for a long time after, and not the kind of baby you seem to crave, either. It comes back on him now and again. It's what he has to live with. You'd have to live with it, too."

"You can't scare me with that kind of talk." She bent over him from the height of the porch, scolding him with bared teeth and looking for all the world like a marmot defending its cold castle of rocks.

"I won't have to scare you. You'll see it soon enough. Especially after I start asking questions like, 'How many years can you stand to be this far from California?'"

He lifted his face, waiting for the hot string of curses to come. But Charlotte whisked herself into the house faster than he had imagined she could, her face blotchy and disarrayed. Had he really frightened her? He hoped to hell he had.

He went to his truck and reached under the seat for a shiny, unopened bottle of vodka. He cracked the seal on the bottle and drove to the trailer near Baggs and stayed all afternoon with the woman who lived there. He paid double her usual fee, though it took all of her backseat skill to rouse him even once. He emerged at twilight into a gloomy silence that was broken only by the harsh commands of a flock of migrating geese. The high, frail arrow of birds passed over him and over the trailer whose windows were becoming mirrored with the evening's frost. He wished he had a shotgun. He wished he could disrupt the loud certainty of those birds. Instead, he could only watch them rise and fade into the approaching night like the rising and fading of windborne ash.

It was Buren who developed a scheme to break the logjam. But Adams knew he was using Buren's deviousness for his own reasons. Because he was tired of the tension and the lack of sleep. Because he was tired of fighting about the alcohol and, now, the smell of marijuana that lingered in the machine shed in the mornings. Because Hobbs was red-eyed and losing weight and spending more and more time looking over his burned shoulder for things nobody else could see. Adams knew he had been wrong to challenge his sister's fortitude. He had only inspired Charlotte to dig in her heels. There was no way she was going to leave the Trumpet Bell until the choice was hers to make. But he didn't believe she really wanted to be a ranch wife. She just wanted to prove her independence. According to Buren, that meant C.D. Hobbs was the one they would have to pry loose first.

"Separation is the key," Buren said, from his office in Cheyenne. "The supposed mutual love will vanish like smoke once they are apart." Adams imagined his brother mincing out a gesture of separation with his uncallused hands. "I like your idea of getting him some medical help before he goes completely around the bend. Why don't we arrange that? I could come over for a few days. We could work out the details. All it will take is clever timing and a dose of your killer marine instinct."

"Please don't talk about our time in uniform like that."
Adams's words shot away from him before he could cleanse
them of doubt, but he didn't care. Buren was like an epidemic
with his attitudes. Buren lived to spread himself into every corner of other people's lives.

"Rationing the guilt already, are we?"

"You go to hell."

"That's just what I mean," Buren mused. "You're right on
the brink, little brother. Keep yourself there."

So they did it like this on a Saturday in mid-October when the
moon was a fish scale stranded in the lake of the sky. Adams
acquired some dynamite and blasting caps in order to blow out
a beaver dam on Ram Horn Creek. The dam wasn't blocking
much water. It would be a simple job, which was why Adams
told Omero he could take the day off to visit his sick sister up
in Hanna. Hobbs could help. Omero looked away when Adams
said that. Omero knew it wasn't possible to work with Hobbs
and explosives. Hobbs couldn't tolerate the noise.

Buren asked Hobbs to take a slow walk along the creek so
they could discuss insurance and licenses, the things a lawyer
understands when it comes to marriage. The collies, Nan and
Sol, accompanied them, casting ahead at great distances into
the nubbed fabric of greasewood and sage. The brothers didn't
even arrange a signal. Adams had buried two charges at the
base of the dam. He waited until he heard the sermonizing of
Buren's voice, then he lit the green twist of fuses. Buren would
later recall the uncolored fire of the falling sun and the complete absence of wind. "Everything was at a pause," he told
Adams, "just waiting for you."

Swish, boom. Swish, boom. The explosions sounded so
much like mortar fire that Adams himself went clammy with
sweat. The two geysers of sound were followed by a dark rain
of willow twigs and mud. Adams had sheltered himself behind some deadfall timber. He emerged when he heard what
he thought was a genial shout from his brother. Sure enough,
Buren and Hobbs were a safe distance from the blast site. They

looked startled, but not injured. Yet once Hobbs saw his old gun-crew leader scuttle from the shadows, Adams's arms and legs slick with mud, his body in a military charge, he swung all the way back on his pendulum. He fell to his knees and began to tear at one of his eyeballs with both hands. He screamed that the eye was burning into his brain like a brand.

They had to restrain him. They had to tie his hands and feet together with their belts. Buren seemed hypnotized by the symphonic madness that seized Hobbs, the way the famously reticent Hobbs shrieked about needing the bright lights turned off, needing to *know*. Adams was not hypnotized. The suffering scalded him just as it had twenty-five years before. He had trouble catching his breath. His ears drummed with his pulse. What the hell had he done? At Chosin, he had cradled Hobbs in his arms as a bloody-fisted corpsman stuck him with one last ampule of morphine. He'd fought, with Spoonhauer and the few men from Easy Company who hadn't died or disappeared, for ten more snow-blind days to keep from falling into the hands of the Chinese. And for what? So he and Hobbs could relive that past hell moment when their souls had first gone to cinder? He pinned Hobbs's head between his muddy knees to keep him from pounding it to pulp.

"It's okay," he said. "It's going to be okay." But it wasn't okay. His hands stank from handling the dynamite, from pressing the detonating caps into its cake-like flesh. The smell of his hands made him want to vomit.

No, howled Hobbs. *No no nobody live no.*

Buren's face looked as dented as a water pail. "Well, I never. . . . This is . . . dramatic. What do we do?"

"It's what we should have done in the first place," Adams croaked as Hobbs's lower legs wriggled against the ground like a smashed fly's. "Jesus. Don't you see it? We're the real cowards here. I swear to god we are. Honest men, real men, would have killed him straight out."

Charlotte didn't allow for the high arcing of grief. She went right to the marrow of blame, whole years of it. They couldn't quiet Hobbs enough to drive him to the hospital in Rawlins, so Charlotte saw all too well what they'd wrought after they hauled Hobbs to the ranch yard in the back of Adams's truck where they waited for the volunteer ambulance from Baggs.

"He'll be fine," Buren told her after she rushed from the house. "There was a little accident, but there aren't any wounds. He just needs to be tranquilized." Charlotte scrambled into the truck bed where Adams was still holding Hobbs's head in his lap. Hobbs's bound legs struggled to run, and the veins in his neck were bruise-colored from the pressure of the terror in his blood. The open eye was maybe the worst. It rolled cloudy and blind like the eye of a wild horse Adams had once found trapped in barbed wire near Mexican Flats. The horse had been tangled in the wire for days. The fly eggs in its torn hide had cycled into feeding maggots.

"I heard an explosion." There was a careful query in Charlotte's voice. "Did a charge go off early?"

But Adams had no more lies to seal over his lips. He took the dish towel his sister held in her hands and tried to soak up the urine that stained the front of Hobbs's jeans.

"It was a little accident," Buren repeated.

"Nothing about you has ever been an accident," she sneered. And as the realization of how far gone Hobbs was began to sink in, Charlotte began to curse them both. She screamed at Buren about impotence and his insipid worship of money. She called him a faggot and a foul, Nixon-loving soul. But Adams was the one she struck, lashing at his unaverted face with the palm of her hand again and again while he knelt over the trembling Hobbs.

"You're afraid of everything that matters," she spit. "I can't believe it. I'd believe anything of that turd," she said, meaning Buren, "but you, there are a million ways you could have been better. You're not even normal anymore, Fremont. You're afraid of love—mine and everybody else's. You're afraid of what C.D. and I might build out here on your Dead Sea of nothing. You hate women and happiness and every damn thing that's different from you." She paused, her eyes and nose streaming with tears and snot, her breathing throttled by deep, vibrating sobs. Her quarantined eyes focused on his face, and she struck him again, more bone than palm this time. He wanted to grab her small, freckled hand and hold it safe in his own like he'd once held the small, panicked sparrows that fell from their nests among the willows by the creek. But he didn't do it. Charlotte was punishment. C.D. Hobbs was not the only test he'd failed.

When the ambulance arrived, a paramedic shot up Hobbs with a sedative. Buren told the paramedic, without interruption, about Hobbs's mental history and made the suggestion that he be bound over to the veterans hospital in Salt Lake once the doctors in Rawlins got him stable. Adams said only that he would follow the ambulance in his own truck. Charlotte, to his surprise, declined to make the journey even in the ambulance. When Adams returned to the Trumpet Bell at two in the morning he found Buren trying to read a book in the parlor. The rims of Buren's eyes were red and pooled with self-pity. He was also weak-kneed from borrowed vodka. Charlotte, he said, was gone. She'd taken her sea bag out the door before sunset. She claimed she'd called a man from Wamsutter to come get her, and Buren could confirm that she had climbed into somebody's covered pickup not long after she reached the end of the driveway. He had watched her with binoculars. She'd left them both a message, Buren said. Adams asked to hear it.

"She says she's off to sow ruin in the world since that's all she's ever learned from her brothers." Buren was still wearing the binoculars. He smeared at the lenses with his fingers. "She says we've left her with nothing but bad memories and the ability to spread her legs."

Adams stared at his older brother who sat in the dim aura of a shaded lamp. Buren had somehow managed to shower and shave before his communion with the vodka. The effort struck Adams as despicable.

"Is there a baby?" Adams asked.

"She didn't say." Buren sucked on his pickled lips in a way that made him look fussy and old. "We may never know. She said she was remaking our mother's wedding dress. She took the fabric with her. The one thing we can state with certainty is that those two were long on fantasy and hope."

"And we're not?" Adams heaved the question at his brother like it was a heavy piece of furniture. "We don't live that way anymore? Is she right? Is Charlotte god damn right?"

Buren looked at him with a sliver left to each drunken eye. "I think you should select an answer to those questions you can live with, Fremont. I have. I don't expect you and I will imitate each other's mistakes quite this way again."

IV

Trumpet Bell Land & Sheep Company

Baggs, Wyoming

1995

HOBBS SPENT HOURS SNIPPING METAL AT HIS WORK-bench. This devotion spooked Adams. He thought it might be better for them both if they focused on less eccentric behaviors, so he was in the house, trying to register them for a weed-and-seed seminar, when the phone rang. The call was from a woman who said she was with the veterans post in Rawlins. She called herself Sugar. Adams had never heard of her. The VFW had stopped calling him years ago because he'd asked them to leave him out of things. When the woman asked for Hobbs, Adams was startled. He still thought of Hobbs as a man who rarely left footprints in the world. But he took a message. He gave the message to Hobbs, who didn't look surprised even though he never got phone calls.

"W-we could go to town on Tuesday," Hobbs said. "Get up there. Have some lunch."

"We could. But I don't go to the post. The boys out of Vietnam talk too much."

"Maybe I could borrow the F-f-ford," Hobbs said, referring to the only vehicle they had that was dependable enough to make the trip. "If you thought that was a option."

It occurred to Adams that a change of scenery might be just the ticket. A trip to Rawlins and exposure to other people, regular people, might be better than chores when it came to taking Hobbs's mind off his little doll workshop. He said, "It's something to think about. I'd be willing to chauffeur you to the VFW for all the sliced roast beef and gossip you can stand. But I won't come in. I'll find my own way to waste time."

Tuesday morning broke with clouds as low as the barn roof. Adams could feel the knife edge of a hovering cold front in his knees. But the drive north on the two-lane to Creston Junction was uneventful. Kerchiefs of snow wrapped themselves around the truck and turned the interior blue with shadow, but the visibility stayed good. On the interstate, they passed several semis that had been blown over on their sides by high wind the night before. They didn't worry. The pavement was clear. Even an eighty-mile-an-hour gust wasn't going to roll the heavy Ford.

The city of Rawlins looked hunkered down to Adams. Its plowed streets were the same gravel beige color as the surrounding hills. He could remember when Rawlins felt striving and expectant, when it was more than enough town for him and everybody he knew. These days Rawlins was more about hanging on than striving.

"Sure you won't come in?" Hobbs asked as Adams swung onto Cedar Street.

"Not in a million, buddy. You have a good time."

Hobbs stepped out of the heated cab into the nail taps of fresh, hard sleet. The way he hefted his shoulders into the weather gave Adams a jolt. Why was his friend so energized by the prospect of eating lunch in a windowless, sauerkraut-smelling hall with a bunch of strangers? Surely Hobbs wasn't going to the post to drink. Drinking was easy there, and cheap, and there was always company. He cursed himself for not considering the possibility earlier. How stupid could he be? It would be a hell of a time for them both if Hobbs slipped into that tunnel.

He lit a cigarette and mulled over his options. He could follow Hobbs like a mother hen. He could park across from the VFW and pretend to keep an eye on things. He could go for his own hot lunch at Rose's, where the Mexican food was worth the hour drive from home. Or he could give Hobbs some rope and head to the lumberyard and buy the supplies he needed to replace the kitchen floor. The old floor, with its buckled corners and cigarette burns, had become a recent source of embarrassment to him. Despite the weird moments, Hobbs's reappearance on the ranch was changing how he saw the things in his life and the way he lived among them. He'd been squatting in the cave of his bachelorhood for too long. It was time to crawl out of that cave. Young Sam Gunderson had laid the current kitchen linoleum twenty years before as part of a barter deal for hay. Replacing it was just the sort of thing he and C.D. should do.

The do-it-yourself center at the lumberyard, which heralded budget optimism at every turn, was the sort of place he hated. But it had what he needed—backing paper, adhesive, scrapers, trowels, and too many patterns of vinyl flooring to choose from. He selected a pattern that was lighter and simpler than the corn-colored mosaic Sam Gunderson had installed. He didn't ask many questions, and he didn't leave much room for the sales clerk, an acned young man with fox-red hair, to offer advice, though he thanked him for his help as they loaded his purchases into the open bed of the Ford. He drove to the parking lot of the VFW with the truck's exhaust rising and twitching behind him like the tail of an impatient animal. He was late.

Hobbs was waiting for him in the recessed door of the veterans post. His hands were jammed into the pockets of his caramel jacket, and he was stomping his work boots to keep his feet warm. There was a woman with him, undoubtedly the so-called Sugar. Sugar, Adams soon found out, had lost a brother in Vietnam and was married to a guy who'd done twenty solid years in the navy. She organized social events for the post. Hobbs started talking about her as soon as he got into the truck. He talked while Adams scrutinized the woman through the windshield. Sugar, sometimes called Shug, was small and stubbornly underdressed in Wranglers and a denim jacket embroidered with a POW/MIA flag. Her face, what he could see of it, was lived in but not unattractive. She had short, black, overdyed hair, and he could track the sashay of her eyes even from a distance. Adams guessed she was a good dancer, the kind he'd spun in and out of his arms many times in the past. She wore lots of rings on her fingers. Her lipstick was as orange as a highway flare. For a moment, Adams was sure he knew Sugar from somewhere—she was that familiar. When she lifted both hands to wave good-bye to Hobbs, he knew he recognized her only as a kind of ghost. It had been that long since he'd looked at a woman with interest. The realization made him laugh.

"What's so funny?" Hobbs asked.

"That gal," Adams said. "Looks like she's got voltage."

"She's m-married," Hobbs said.

"'Course she's married, that's part of what makes it funny. I'm finally old enough to enjoy being reminded I'm a fool."

"You want me to call her over here?"

"No. She looks as good as she ever will from this distance. I'm glad she's friendly."

"You'd like her. I hadn't thought about it, b-but you would. I d-do."

"I know," Adams said, and he kept some of the resonance of his remark to himself, for himself.

They made good time on the highway as part of a trickle of vehicles hoping to reach the desert promise of Nevada or California despite the lousy forecast. The horizon was a spume of cloud the color of burning oil. Adams reckoned it had been more than five years since he'd been farther west than Salt Lake City, though he felt no regret about that fact. Hobbs asked him what was loaded in the back of the truck, and he told him.

"I might need some help on the floor job. It's straight grunt work, but the scraping and measuring will make me more of a S.O.B. than usual."

"I been a grunt."

"Yeah, you have, but you're top hand now, C.D. I mean it. This is my own kind of house thing. I've neglected that house. You don't have to pitch in."

Hobbs dropped his chin toward his chest.

"I don't mean to leave you out, if you're willing," Adams continued. "I'd be lying if I said I couldn't use you."

Hobbs sat bolt upright in his seat, as if he'd been called to attention. The prospect of a shared project pleased him. He asked if Adams wanted to hear about the meeting at the post, and Adams said he did as long as the telling was worth a cigarette. Adams looped the truck off the interstate at the Baggs exit without much reduction in speed, driving one-handed the way they'd both learned from Uncle Gene. Hobbs lit them Winstons, not his regular brand.

"It was nice," Hobbs said. "Hot f-food, plenty of that. Beef—like you said—and beans and salad. You could have white b-bread or brown. No beer. That's a lunch rule they've just started. I met two guys who guard at the prison. They served in th-that Desert Storm."

"See anybody you know?" Adams didn't want to hear about some dogface's vacation in the Gulf.

"Ruth Colbert's brother. Remember how he b-broke his leg in the wild-horse race at county fair? He d-don't even have a limp." Hobbs paused, tugged his pants down over his boot tops. "The Nam guys is getting old. That's part of what Shug wants to t-talk to me about, if I had advice."

"She think you were Vietnam?" Most of the gray hair Hobbs had was crowded at his temples. And people never remembered Korea. The Korean War was more forgotten than the Vietnam one they'd lost.

"Naw. I told her I was full-scale senior citizen. She's only fifty-three."

"Whoa. You got that far with her?"

Hobbs lathed up a grin. "Going to t-town brings out the devil in you, Fremont."

"And that ain't news, is it?"

"Guess not," Hobbs said, shaking his head. "N-not if we count all the past times." Then he got quiet like he was about to summon up a longer speech.

"Don't even think it," Adams said. "I told you I don't go to the post, and I don't. Drive to town whenever you want. You can take this truck. Say howdy to Sugar and all the rest. But I'm not in the mix. If you bother me about it again, I'll ask a question you don't want to answer."

"What's that?" Hobbs swung his head in Adams's direction. His eyes had a filmy, condensed look.

Adams thought of winged spirits and spaceships, but he suddenly couldn't bring himself to take his own bait. It seemed wrong to bring up the stories Hobbs was trying to retell with his little figurines. The whole point of going to Rawlins was to ease the pressure of those stories. "Well, for instance, just for speculation, I could ask for a complete list of all the ladies in your life."

Hobbs clamped his lips and stared at the wet end of his half-smoked cigarette. He didn't seem to know whether Adams's comment was meant to be funny or mean. Adams didn't know, either. He'd dodged one pit only to fall into another.

They didn't speak for nearly twenty miles. Hobbs eventually recovered enough to count the steers he could see in the rubbed-out pastures owned by the absentee Coloradan who'd bought the Barnheisel spread after Steve cashed out to live with his daughter in Casper. The black fang of Battle Mountain came into view to the south, drawing them over the Continental Divide and into the open mouth of home. Adams welcomed the sight of his ice-stitched pastures and the rusty stanchion of Bell Butte. He felt bad about what he'd said to Hobbs. He hadn't meant to pour cold water on the man's enthusiasms; he just wanted Hobbs to stay connected to the real world. He wondered again if the VFW might be a bad idea. What if Sugar or somebody sprayed with the same kind of sweet perfume asked Hobbs the wrong kind of questions about his war?

When they got back to the Trumpet Bell, Hobbs went onto the porch to release the dogs from the mudroom where Adams had allowed them to stay because of the cold. The young dogs, Zeke and Dan, bolted from the house and leaped into the truck bed, their sinewy, thick-furred bodies taut with frustration because they'd been left behind. Rain ambled onto the porch and stretched his dappled legs in a slash of sunlight before he joined in a long moment of communion with Hobbs.

As Adams carried his smaller purchases into the house, he smelled the hot salt smell of dog urine. It came from the corner of the mudroom where he'd left the dogs a pair of old blankets. Surely the piss came from Rain, and surely it was a bad sign. A dog that couldn't control himself was a dog you had to take behind the barn and shoot. The idea of losing Rain rifled across Adams's heart. He dreaded that day. Rain had been with him a long time. But it was the way of this country to kill a creature when it could no longer take care of itself.

They tore up the old kitchen floor and hauled the pieces to the trash pit behind the barn. They scraped at the tarlike adhesive, and while they were doing that, Adams decided to re-floor the mudroom as well. He suspected he was rolling down a steep slope because a new floor would make the kitchen cabinets look dingy, and if they repainted the cabinets, the walls and battered gas stove would look like shit. But what the hell? He and Hobbs needed the challenge. He reminded himself of that.

Hobbs did a meticulous job measuring sections of new floor with a T square and pencil. He made himself a kind of bible-school necklace from knotted fishing line and lead sinkers, and he liked to wear the long strands of the necklace even though it sometimes got in his way as they worked. He seemed mostly calm and unprophetic, though he did talk to himself quite a bit. The conversations were animated and, in Hobbs's mind, two-sided.

"He likes what we're doing," he said to Adams after they glued down the first shiny square of linoleum.

"What? Who?"

"You know. H-him." Hobbs glanced up at the ceiling. "He approves of everything you do."

Adams decided to play along. "Good. That satisfies me. I could use some approval."

Hobbs nodded. "I know."

"Give him my thanks, will you?" Adams pressed his hands onto the new piece of flooring to make sure it was set.

Hobbs nodded again. "I already have."

Hobbs had stopped manufacturing his little people. This was a relief to Adams. The workbench looked the same each morning—dusty, half populated, on hiatus. He peered out his uncurtained kitchen windows into a depthless blue sky, and he felt something akin to hope. The air was varnished with the sheer and brittle light he'd known all his life, a promised heat that once again awakened desires he'd learned to lift out

of himself and examine. He thought he understood brittleness
now, how a man could crack and piece himself back together.
There were ways to blend permanence and pain—he truly believed that.

Late one afternoon, when he scraped his knuckles working under the toe kick of the cabinets, Adams glimpsed an old
memory that hurdled itself away from him like a startled pheas-
ant. The memory came into focus as he sucked on the raw ooze
of his own skin, tasting salt. Something to do with a pair of
lambs and an overhang of scrub juniper near Mount Zirkel.
Something almost forgotten. He had yanked the twin lambs to
safety that day as their sag-bellied mother bawled from the top
of the cliff. He was lucky he hadn't dropped them or dislocated
their shoulders. It was a maneuver that cost him the skin on
the back of his hands. He was thirteen, and it was the last time
he left summer camp without his gloves. Old Etchepare hadn't
bothered to praise him or tell him he was stupid as they sat
together next to the cook's tent. Adams soaked his hands in
a stew pot of soapy water to get the sting out of them, and
the boss herder never spoke. Old Etch didn't believe judgment
came with words.

"There is this one thing with the sheep," Old Etch told him.
It was later in both their lives, Adams back from his war, Old
Etchepare carrying a tumor in his gut that rode in front of him
like an unborn child. "A man who move the band, he go *out* in
the world like you know. He walk, see a thing around him here
and around him there." Etch spread his gnarled fingers. "Man
who beds sheep at end of the day, the world come *to* that man.
Sometime, he find what other ones never wait for."

On the third afternoon of floor work, Adams drove down to
Baggs to buy vitamins for the horses. The stink of vinyl and adhesive had gotten to him, making his head feel empty and light.
He wanted a break. He left Hobbs sharpening the teeth of the
mower blade on the grinder in the shed. Baggs was the same
as ever—good for postage stamps and a paint-stripping cup of

coffee. When he drove back into the ranch yard, the collies, Dan and Zeke, streaked right for him. He saw the porch door slam itself against the blistered gray siding of the house. The dogs shouldn't have been indoors. They kept their heads low and obedient as he greeted them. Strangely, their flanks were trembling. Inside, Adams found Hobbs sitting on the bright new kitchen floor, his belly and thighs ribboned with blood. Rain was huddled against him.

"You," Hobbs gasped, the whites of his eyes huge and skittish, "you didn't want dogs in here."

Adams chose the slow approach because he knew something about the scene was very bad. He set the jar of vitamins on the countertop and closed the door between the mudroom and kitchen, damming the icy flow of air. He could see the fog of his breath, and the rising breath of Hobbs and the panting Rain. When he first approached Hobbs, Rain growled deep in his throat and showed his teeth, but Adams put a stop to that with a quiet word. Hobbs had both hands cradled against his gut. Adams could see blood that was both dry and wet.

"How bad is it? You lose a finger on the mower?"

"N...no."

Adams didn't like the fish belly color of Hobbs's face or the way he couldn't seem to fill his lungs. He wondered about a heart attack. "Let me see."

Hobbs lifted his left arm and rotated it from front to back as if it was on a skewer.

The damage ran from the center of the palm up toward the elbow. Above the wrist was a dark line of exposed meat shaped like a hook. If arteries had been cut, Adams couldn't see the pulsing. One of the curved linoleum knives was on the floor near the refrigerator. It was smeared with blood that had turned thick and brown in the cold.

"Try . . . try to help. Then . . . h-he came so fast . . . and Rain goes. . . ." The words were short and shallow. Panicked.

"Slow yourself down. We don't got a train to catch. Does it hurt much?"

Hobbs nodded. Portions of the cut were deep, but it wasn't going to kill anybody, so Adams stayed with his worry about Hobbs's heart.

"I want to wrap it in something clean, take you to town to see the doc."

Hobbs's left leg went rigid. The other leg flexed as if something was snaking inside it. Adams knelt closer, touching Hobbs's elbow with both hands, feeling how cold his skin was against Hobbs's. "I don't mean a hospital, C.D., not like that. Just stitches and a antibiotic."

"You do it." The blued eyes rolled upward in their sockets, spooked and unforgiving at the same time. Adams had to look away.

"Oh, hell. Don't make me—" But what could he promise that Hobbs would believe when it came to doctors? He'd burned that damn bridge a long time ago. "What were you doing, C.D.? You didn't have to work in here without me. We're not in a hurry, and you—"

"P-please."

"Jesus, then. Jesus Christ. Can you move your fingers, all five of them, because if you can't move your fingers, I'm not touching you." He knew he'd turned the corner as soon as he opened his mouth. He couldn't say exactly what had taken him around the turn, but it was happening. He was going to do whatever it took to keep Hobbs from going off the deep end. He held Hobbs's arm at the bicep and watched the flat, glistening sheath of a tendon slide under the gap of the wound. It reminded him of a ewe he'd once found in Lame Jack Gulch. Coyotes had ripped at her right hind Achilles until you could see exactly how it worked.

Hobbs slumped against the kitchen wall. He appeared exhausted. And grateful. There was dried spit at the corners of his mouth. "I got to get the kit from the barn," Adams said. "You be all right for a minute?"

Hobbs gave half a nod. His eyelids were closed, but Adams could see that his eyes were moving left, then right, as if they were tracking something small and slow in the distance. "Is there anything else going on, C.D? Does your chest hurt? Your head? Did you see something that made you. . . ." He paused to lick at his lips. "Shit, did you cut yourself without meaning to? I don't want to make a mistake here."

"Hurt my neck." The sealed eyes were still moving, like ball bearings in grease.

"Huh?"

"You . . . hurt my neck."

Adams crouched next to Hobbs again, dread shaping itself into an iron band around his chest. He used his thumbs to probe both sides of Hobbs's throat. There were no cuts or nicks there, only a reddish smudge that might be the beginning of a bruise. The fishing line necklace was no longer draped around the collar of Hobbs's shirt. Adams wondered about that. When he spotted the necklace looped like pigging string around one of Hobbs's belt loops, he wondered even more. Had Hobbs seen something, imagined something, that led him to take a whack at his own throat? Jesus, that was a black thought. And if he was aiming at his throat, how had he sliced his arm instead?

"Fix it, Fremont. She says you don't have to fix everything, you just got to try." Now the voice was as firm and polished as a teacher's apple. It scared him.

"Hang on there, bud. I'm going to the barn." Adams's own words cracked against one another like finger bones. He tried to maintain his poise as he headed for the door.

He had the basics in his medical kit. Heavy silk thread. Suture needles. Wide, sterile bandages meant for the horses. He could put in enough stitches to make it look good, then talk Hobbs into having somebody else sew it up right. He could do it. But should he? Was he already too late? He found himself jogging out of the barn, his arms full of more supplies than he'd ever need. He just wanted it to stop. He wanted Hobbs to be the way he used to be, the way he'd been that very morning when they ate pancakes for breakfast. He wanted Hobbs to be normal. When he got back to the house, he found Rain licking blood from the floor. Hobbs had toppled onto his side and squeezed himself into a tight ball.

He was afraid he knew what Hobbs was thinking down there in his roly-poly ball. Hobbs was thinking that Fremont Adams was fresh out of excuses. If he could stitch the female parts back inside a ewe that had been turned inside out by a bad labor, he could handle a knife cut on a man's arm. Fremont Adams could save him. Pain was never a reason to avoid a thing that had to be done.

He put what he needed on a plastic dinner plate. Then he unzipped the quilted jacket he'd worn to Baggs, though he didn't take it off. He removed his knit hat, and he washed his hands twice, scrubbing at the fingernails before he squatted between Hobbs and the row of cabinets that held their pots and pans. He conceded the other side to Rain, who laid himself along the hunch of Hobbs's spine with his grizzled head facing the door. Rain kept looking at that door, ears peaked, eyes shining, like he was waiting for something big and loud to come right through it.

Adams rolled up Hobbs's stained sleeves, first one, then the other. "I might have to talk myself through this, C.D. Blue Pete always had to talk when he did something, remember?" Hobbs didn't respond, so he applied a wet towel to the skin, refolding the towel as it absorbed blood. He'd seen head wounds bleed like this. They always looked worse than they were. He was glad when the hot, clean water seemed to unbind Hobbs a little. "Blue Pete never had his hands clean as this, did he? That man was a walking buffalo wallow." Although Adams wasn't able to make Hobbs speak or laugh, he was able to sit him back against the wall with his left elbow resting atop his knees. It was just like soothing a horse, he thought as he bathed the skin until the dried blood began to come off in flakes. You had to get comfort and trust moving in the same direction, flowing like a stream.

He made a kind of surgical table on his own lap and opened the dusty pack of needles, then the envelopes of coiled thread. He could feel Hobbs watching him. When he swabbed the arm with disinfectant, the color and smell made him think of Uncle Gene and all the injured animals they'd tried to put back together with their own hands. They'd played veterinarian to save money. And they'd never healed as many of their patients as they hoped.

Adams doused a hemostat with disinfectant and lined up the marbled edges of the cut as well as he could. "I'm sewing more skin than muscle," he told Hobbs. "I think I can get the stitches to hold, but they'll be hard to keep tight. You'll have to stay real still, even when it hurts." Hobbs flinched when the hemostat was clamped in, but Adams kept his pace and drove the needle through one flap of skin and then the other. The first stitch was lopsided and a little loose. When he tied off the second stitch, he felt rather than heard Hobbs begin to weep. The weeping moved from Hobbs's body into his own with the same vibrations as the growl of an animal.

His own fingertips became brown with disinfectant. When he paused to soak up more blood, he could see those fingers tremble from effort. So much effort. There was sobbing now from Hobbs, the hot current of it pouring onto Adams's shoulder where Hobbs had pressed his face. There were high-pitched whines from Rain, too. They flailed into his ears.

"Why don't you open your eyes, C.D., and make a guess. I'm thinking twenty stitches will do her. What do you think?" His words—which were meant to comfort—didn't change anything. Hobbs kept the bones of his arm flat and motionless. The stitches gathered like black barbs on a fence. But Hobbs was suffering, and Adams couldn't escape the sense that he was sewing them both to a fate they'd hoped to avoid. "I suppose you got me right where you want me, huh—doctoring on you like you're a piece of stock. After everything that's happened with us, you probably think it makes sense, that this is as far as I've got." He spoke with a tongue that tasted of bad meat. "I don't blame you, you know. You bear no blame. So here's my question: Why does it all keep coming back on us? You seem to be reliving . . . well, you seem to be remembering how I came after you on that Korea hill. What I did. I want to make it right, but why does it keep coming back? And why do you bring other people—like my sister or the boys from Easy

Company—into what's between us when they're away from here or dead, and we're just on our own?"

There were no words from Hobbs. No motion. Adams tied off another small, tight knot.

"Should a man turn around to face his wrongs, or should he try to make a good life from what's in front of him? Which is the right way to live? That's where I'm stuck, C.D. That's the answer I need from you."

Hobbs rolled against him, quaking, covering his swollen face with his uncut hand. Rain got to his feet to guard them all against whatever he believed was on the other side of the door. Adams could see a slickness amid the dog's belly fur. The dog had pissed himself, bad. The silver hemostat shook itself free of Adams's hand when he saw that.

"A answer," he whispered, recalling the nothingness he'd emerged from after the Chinese mortar shell had erased all light and sound on Hill 1281. That shell had erased him, too, in a lot of ways. It had vaporized the self he was so sure of. He'd never shared with Hobbs the damning truths he'd learned after Chosin: how a battalion surgeon had seen Sutherland in a group of prisoners wired together by the Chinese, how Pilcher's frozen body had been dumped in a shallow trench grave because the marines had no way to retreat with their dead. "I don't know why I do what I do to you," he said. "There's no thinking to it. That knife—the Baker one—I lost it, you know. I left it with the medic who tried to help us. He said . . . he said I should hold onto you. He wasn't ever coming down from there, and I left him the knife. A lot of us never came down from there." His mind began to crowd with all the words and syllables he might finally say out loud. He felt as though a skin far below his real skin had been punctured, and he was going to have to say certain words if he wanted to survive the rupture. He tried to go on. "What do you think a selfish, unthinking son of a bitch can really fix?" He realized he was staring at the pink glaze of what had once been Hobbs's right ear, addressing it. "I've done you wrong, more than once. I can't see how to fix that."

Hobbs tightened himself back into a ball, the suture thread scrawled across his wrist like an unfinished signature. He began to breathe like a man grappling with sleep. When Adams tried to clear his own eyes, he saw his dog, Rain, through a wet, warping haze. The dog was standing upright, still and judgmental and careful. And the dog held his own question in a pair of spackled eyes: What kind of lifelong casualty was John Fremont Adams willing to be?

He does it when the house is his alone. Hobbs has been bandaged, covered with blankets, and left to rest in his room in the shed. They've eaten a meal of buttered spaghetti decorated with peas from a can. They've gotten back to the surface of normal, if there is such a thing. Hobbs's footfalls are delicate. He carries his head slightly to one side as if his neck is strained, but his pupils are stark and clear, the color of pond water under ice. When he's finally by himself in the parlor, Adams realizes it's almost the spring equinox. A beveled light breaches the parlor windows, and he knows if he stands close to the unwashed glass he will see the citrus plume of the sun disappear behind the black rampart of Skull Rim. Soon there will be heat and thaw. Long spring rains will fall upon his welcoming fields. This used to be what he waited for. When he was a man birthing lambs, a man who directed mountain runoff into his neighbors' dry canals, he wanted each year to begin again. Now he doesn't understand what he's waiting for, or whether it's worth waiting at all.

She says you don't got to fix everything, you just got to try. The words settle on his shoulders like heavy droplets of fog. Chilled. Encompassing. He's on the phone before he even thinks about it. He grips the receiver, contemplating the roar in his ears that comes partly from the clamoring fire in the stove and partly from the haste of his heart as the operator gives him a number for Charlotte Adams. Buren once tracked their sister to Denver. He says she works at a frame shop in the old downtown. The operator repeats the number as he copies it in pencil on a clean piece of typing paper drawn from the center drawer

of his mother's walnut desk. He thanks the operator, grateful
he has received the information from a human voice. 970 . . .
381. . . . The numerals march and retreat before his eyes. He
needs to turn the lamp on. He needs to find his reading glasses.
He needs to hang on a moment, breathe, make sure his priori-
ties are in a long, straight line. He tells himself not to talk about
the ranch and how it's cratered, she won't give a fig about that.
Let her tell about a husband, or a man if she has one, don't
take the lead there. Say hello, damn it. Be polite. Talk about
Hobbs, mention Hobbs early because that's why you're calling,
isn't it?

Isn't it?

He punches the number pads with his forefinger, and the
phone squawks its unpitched tune. His hands are icy. Sweat
curdles under his arms and belt while the phone lines shiver
and click, and then Charlotte's end begins to ring—hollow, distant, as empty as a culvert. What if he gets one of those infernal machines? What if he gets a man's voice? He's thinking
hard about that, girding himself as her phone continues to ring
until that's what he does get. The words of a man.

Don't do it 'cause of me.

The words ride above the racing of his blood like birds above
the waves of the sea.

Put it down. She.

Don't do it for me.

Hobbs lifts the receiver from Adams's damp hand and places
it in its hard, black cradle. Where has he come from?

"Sorry," Hobbs says. He's standing there with a blaze orange hunter's cap on his head, his two-day beard giving a char-
coal blur to every part of his face except the lit circuits of his
eyes. He holds his bandaged arm close to his body as if it is a
package, and he looks weary through the backbone, as weary
as Adams feels. There is something slightly shrunken about
him, too, a containment that is unfamiliar. It is the stance of a
man who is looking for forgiveness. Or punishment.

"How'd you know?"

"Wish I could tell you, Fremont."

"It's my business."

Hobbs shakes his head. "More hers."

Adams's blood coils between his lungs and heart. It tests its lash on him, striking a sharp pulse in his neck. He has to ask himself whether Hobbs is really ever sorry for anything.

"Coffee?" Hobbs points toward the kitchen.

"So we can sit and talk? I already got your point."

Hobbs steers wide of him and gets to the coffeepot, which he fills with tap water. He's wearing Adams's sheepskin coat, unbuttoned. Its sleeves run almost as long as his fingers. The sight of the coat, which is something Hobbs has never asked to borrow, makes Adams wonder whether forgiveness and punishment might be the same thing to a man with flint sparks in his eyes.

"Don't you think it's interesting how a ranching man is always looking for things? I found the seven pound bolt cutters the other morning, been looking forever. They were in the cab of the big tractor, right behind the seat."

Adams wants to walk into the kitchen and get two coffee mugs out of the cabinet and do the regular duet. But Hobbs's ministry makes him feel balloon-headed, like he's waking up from a long sleep. He hasn't been himself since . . . since he doesn't know when.

"I always lose things. You used to tell me that as a kid." Steam rises from the coffeepot as it percolates over its ring of pure flame. Hobbs shucks the heavy, fleece-lined coat and hangs it on the back of a chair.

"I think we were talking about Charlotte."

"I am," Hobbs says. "You've lost her. I'm trying to tell you we aren't going to get her back."

The blood lash falls again, whipping at him from the inside where he can keep the howling to himself.

"You don't know that."

"Then call her."

"God damn you." Adams drives one of his boots against the parlor floor. Window glass shakes; they both hear it. "You can't tell me what to do about my own sister." And he pivots to where the telephone squats on his mother's walnut desk. But he can't pick it up. It looks ugly to him, peeled and dead. Charlotte hit him in the face the day he stole Hobbs away from her. He feels those blows again—on his sagging, unshaved cheek. Across his eye socket. Harder than ever. Faster.

"I seen her, you know."

Adams halts. He knows he couldn't move now even if he tried. "Wh...what?"

"It weren't that hard. You just have to talk to people when you get off the Denver bus, they're mostly nice about it. You make a certain set of turns on the streets down there, and you can see her. Walk right up."

"She talked to you?"

"She did. Charlotte ain't lost none of her ease with talking. I did surprise her, though."

Adams tries to focus on the door frame between the parlor and the kitchen, anything to give him an anchor. "Bet so."

Hobbs shakes his oranged head while he lays down a pair of napkins and spoons. "She took me out for a sandwich. We both had BLTs, all she had to do was ask her manager. She looks fine. Her boobs are flatter, and she's smaller all the way around but in a good way. She showed me a picture of a little brown girl from down below Mexico that she calls her daughter."

Adams opens his mouth, but that's as far as he's allowed to get. "It's okay," Hobbs says. "There never was no baby. Charlotte says I was shooting blanks. She says she's with a good man now too, though I didn't see no pictures of him. I can tell you the man she's with is not that shop manager. He ain't her type."

And who is? Adams thinks to himself, his heart rolling itself up like a carpet. "She's all right, though? That's what you're saying?"

Hobbs sits himself down at the kitchen table with gusto. He heaps a spoon with sugar. "She's close enough to happy to know what it is. She said it helped her to see me. But she don't want to see you or know about you or Buren in any way. I told her I could change her mind about that."

"I don't think . . ."

"Some things are not yours to decide, Fremont." Hobbs touches his temples with his fingers when he says this. His eyes are closed. "I'm gonna work this my way. Remember that question you asked when you were stitching on me? Sometimes what we done to other people and what we have ahead of us comes together and mixes."

"I don't know if I can believe that," Adams says. He's standing on his whirled floor rug. He's staring at its pattern to nowhere. Charlotte, Charlotte, Charlotte. Even the hushed sounds of her name slice into him. "You do certain things and you can never take them back. Some things don't take a repair. I used to know that. I lived by it like a rule."

"You do live hard and think hard," Hobbs says, sipping. "You got everybody's respect on that. But there's one thing you don't seem to get no matter how many times it's laid out for you. People don't follow your plans. You don't get to choose what returns and what don't. You only get to decide how you'll treat it when it comes."

"You deserve some kind of reward," Buren said. "Both of you. Except I can't imagine what the reward should be. You live on practically nothing."

"We're not going for any kind of prize here," Adams said. "I just want you to know we're getting along good. C.D. wants you to come out and see how we've fixed up the place." He could barely believe he'd made the phone call, particularly because he'd found what he expected to find. Buren was obstreperous and more than a little drunk.

"*Va bene.* I'll answer the Bell."

"Bring some good steaks when you do. I'll cook."

"Can you promise our guest won't hog-tie me to model for his art project?" Orchestral music played behind Buren's lubricated voice. Its sounds faded in and out like the sound of water being moved by a wheel.

Adams swallowed the extra saliva in his mouth. He'd lied about C.D.'s involvement. He was the one who wanted

Buren to come to the ranch. The knowledge that Hobbs had seen Charlotte was suffocating him. He'd been outflanked, outmaneuvered. He wanted to give Hobbs as much reality as he could handle, and to do that he needed help from his brother. "I'm not protecting you from anything, which is the same way I believe you've always treated me. I'm inviting you to dinner."

"At C.D.'s request?"

"Much as he ever makes one," Adams fibbed again. He told Buren a little about the kitchen repairs and nothing about the cut on Hobbs's arm.

"Well. Yes. Do you know the myth of Tantalus? Perhaps C.D. has—"

"Shut up, Buren. I know you've been into the whiskey deep, that's what I *know*. Name a day you'll come out here and take a look at the ranch you still partly own so I can get the hell off the phone."

"Ghosts," Buren said.

Adams waited for the rest of a pronouncement that didn't come. After a delay feather-dusted by music, he gave Buren a nudge. "You might want to fix yourself something with caffeine."

"The reason C.D. is asking for me," Buren said. "It's always about phantoms with him, ghosts alive and dead. We know how he's coping with the dead ones. They're having a gala in your tractor shed. But the living. . . ."

"Just name a day, Buren. Or call me back when you're able."

". . . afraid he'll see her. Charlotte."

Adams felt the bull's-eye strike under the shield of his sternum. He knew all too well which one of them was most afraid of his ghosts. "He's already seen her," he blurted. "Before he showed up here."

The first noise he could distinguish sounded like the thin screaking of a wire against glass. He couldn't imagine how his brother was making that noise.

"Did you hear me, Buren?" Adams couldn't contain his shout.

"Yes. But no. He didn't see Charlotte." Buren cleared his

throat. "Listen to me—he *did not* see her. It's all part of the disintegration."

"I believe him."

"And you want me to come out there to celebrate that fact? Take a good look at yourself, Fremont. You're calling me for assistance. Again. You're asking for support because you know C.D. is pathetic and unsalvageable and, just like last time, you can't take it anymore."

"That's not true," Adams said, trying to separate his anger from a sob. "I got a idea. We'll fix you a nice ranch dinner with the steaks you bring. We'll talk about a few easy things, and C.D. will see we're nothing he can't manage."

"That's not how it'll go, and you know it."

"A day, Buren. Just name a god damn day."

But there was no answer except a kind of low hissing that seemed intended as laughter.

"Fine," Adams said. "I'll take that as a vote for Saturday. Make sure you're here by six."

Adams told Hobbs that Buren was driving out for a meal, nothing more. They used Saturday afternoon to clean the house. Hobbs polished the parlor windows as it began to snow, a feathery, unhurried snow that wasn't likely to foul the roads. Adams stacked wood on the porch as tightly as he might stack stones for a wall, then he mopped the kitchen floor, which didn't need to be mopped. The preparations didn't keep him from being nervous. When they were finished, standing together on the bright, foreign-smelling vinyl in their wool socks, Hobbs asked to borrow a clean shirt. Adams took his best red chamois from a hanger in his closet and gave it to Hobbs, who slipped into his fleece-lined boots to go to the shed where he would bathe himself with the lukewarm water he stored in a thermos. The ranch yard was purple with shadows cast by the same low clouds that cast their silent seeds of snow. Hobbs's trek left black prints in that snow, and he was followed by the dogs who trailed easily behind him, their noses lifted into the muffled quiet.

Buren was punctual, his Buick rocking and whirring its way to the lee side of the horse corral. It was where he always parked. Hobbs was sweeping the porch steps clear of snow for a second time, and he met Buren with a broom in his hands and a shy duck of his uncovered head. Buren wore a tweed jacket and a string tie yoked by a small oval of jade he'd received in appreciation for his years of government lawyering in Cheyenne. If he had boots or an overcoat, he left them in the Buick. Adams met Buren at the door and took from him the paper bags that held steaks and scotch whisky and what felt like an unnecessary bottle of wine. His brother needed a haircut, he could see that much. Rusty white hair wisped over Buren's ears and the high collar of his jacket. But he looked sober enough in the eyes, and his handshake was professionally determined. Adams wondered what it took out of Buren for him to gain control over his sloppiness.

Adams had been frying mushrooms in a skillet, so he went back to it, telling Buren he was welcome to take his jacket off if he saw fit. The kitchen—indeed, the whole house—was as warm as an oven. Buren kept his jacket. He admired the new floor before he stepped onto it with his wet wingtip shoes. "This looks worthy of a wife," he said, a statement of mock praise Adams managed to ignore.

Hobbs asked Buren if he wanted to sit in the parlor, and Buren said yes, so they left Adams to the cooking. Hobbs came back into the kitchen to pour Buren four fingers of scotch over ice. He fixed himself a glass of tap water. Adams unwrapped the thick steaks and seasoned them, trying to eavesdrop on the talk in the parlor. He hadn't thought about what he'd do if the other two started a real conversation without him. Until the sight of the two drinking glasses—one for whisky, one for water—he hadn't thought it might be a possibility.

"He cut it on the mower blade," he shouted, scraping his spatula through the pool of butter in the skillet. "He says he don't need a new tetanus."

There was murmuring from the parlor followed by Buren's legislative voice. "That's what he told me, Fremont. Twice. Now we're talking about a quarter-crack on the roan horse. I didn't know you still had the roan horse. It's a lively time you have out here."

"Yeah," Adams said. "You better believe it."

He tried to stay out of it. He scooped the shrivel of mushrooms onto paper towels and wiped the skillet clean for the steaks. Then he heard laughter. Buren's chuckle was as smooth and deep as their father's. The noise that came from Hobbs was hee-hawing and split. Adams hoped they were making fun of him, trading insults about how bossy and frugal he was, but he knew something else was going on when he made out the name "Shug." He strained his ears until he was certain Buren had asked Hobbs about women, baiting his way up that trail with a series of bad jokes. Buren would latch onto anything Hobbs had to say about a woman. His obnoxious, obsessive loneliness would see to that. And talk about Shug would lead to talk about Charlotte, Adams was sure of it. Buren was definitely looking for trouble.

Adams stepped into the parlor, his spatula held upright so that it dripped steak fat onto his sleeve. He stared at Buren, just stared at him, until he got a response. "C.D. tells me he's joined the inveterate veterans bureaucracy in Rawlins. I asked if he was on a mission to convert you."

"Sounds like I'm missing all the good stories," Adams said. "I sure hate to do that. Could you hold them back until we eat?"

"He knows Sugar," Hobbs said, his water glass resting carefully on both knees. "From his lawyer work. She's told me how proud she is of the protesting she's done in Cheyenne."

Adams knew Buren had never heard of Sugar. He was just trying to ferret out information. Adams wanted to throw his brother out the door, but he badly needed him. That need—which he'd been sanding smooth since he got the idea to invite Buren to dinner—trussed itself tight across his shoulders. He wished to hell he'd been a good enough man to keep the friends he'd once had. Instead, he'd cut them out, ignored them, pretended he only needed himself to be a man. It was a bad fact that Buren was the only person he could turn to for help in this current mess.

They ate at the chrome-legged kitchen table that Hobbs had covered with a square of red-checked oilcloth. Buren went into lecture mode. He talked about his house in Baggs and how it suffered from widely spaced joists and rotting eaves. He talked about the time the three of them had herded sheep together in the mountains as replacements for Francisco who'd been taken in a hay truck to Fort Collins for an emergency operation on a hernia in his balls. It was Uncle Gene's idea to send three boys to replace one invalid man. Buren had not been much help. He was impatient with the sheep and the dogs even though all he had to do was tend camp. The whole topic was designed to make Buren look bad, and it did. Hobbs laughed without caution when Buren recalled the morning he'd lost the entire string of pack animals in the fog.

"That damn mule went off the edge of the trail and took two others with her. Lucky for me my knots didn't hold. It was the only time that son-of-a-bitch Basque ever touched me." Buren smiled, but not with pleasure.

Adams remembered none of it as funny. He and C.D. had stood over the downed mule in a slick black gully of shale, one rifle between them, trying to decide how best to shoot her. Adams had done it, pressing the barrel hard between the mule's frantic eyes. He made himself study the neat hole in her skull and smell the scorched smell of powder and mule hair before they left the carcass for the ravens and the bears. When Old Etch arrived in camp with the week's supplies, he listened to what each boy had to say, then he beat Buren across the ass with his thick belt of Spanish leather until Buren's insolent mouth was out of words. It was the last time Buren went into the mountains.

"Etch cared about mules," Adams said. "Good ones were hard to replace."

"That was his dream world, and he was welcome to it," Buren said, his face heated pink by unexacted revenge. "He was just another of Gene's pathetic projects."

After his second drink and his T-bone steak, Buren told them about the book he was writing. He directed most of his commentary toward Hobbs who listened while Adams stacked dishes. The book was a narrative of the Laury family. It was based on a short, snobbish article Buren had published in a heritage-society magazine in the 1980s. He told them he needed to go to Scotland in order to finish the project. Maybe Ireland as well, if he could find the time. Adams thought about the throng of unfinished family stories he'd heard as a child, the agricultural mishaps and predictable scandals. These were what had attracted Buren's gelid eye. Adams couldn't make himself believe other people would be interested in those ancestral leftovers, but he hadn't seen his poorly shaved brother this enthusiastic about a project since his failed attempt to resurrect the independent weekly newspaper in Baggs, an enterprise that had begun with exaggeration and ended with slander and a single, leaky mimeograph machine. Adams put a box of toothpicks on the wiped oilcloth and made fresh coffee as Buren regaled Hobbs with details of his archival research. Dull as shit, that's what their talk had become. And dullness was the last visitor he'd expected.

Buren rose from the table after half a cup of coffee. The snow, which was accumulating in powdery drifts, gave him an excuse. Adams escorted his brother to the blanketed Buick, offering to sweep the car clean with the straw broom from the porch. As they faced each other under the humming disk of the yard light, which cast its planet rings over the barn and empty corrals, Adams realized that though they had looked nothing alike as boys, age was stamping them with more similarities than he cared to acknowledge. The bony height, the undermined proportions of their cheekbones, the Scots breadth of their hands—he recognized those features from his own bathroom mirror.

"I've never seen him better," Buren said, his cinnamon-colored eyebrows beaded with moisture. "I'll be honest—a trait I rarely favor even with family. I don't believe in a cure for C.D.'s ailments. The state hospital is where he ought to be.

Yet I can't deny the efficacy of this." He waved a hand over his jacketed shoulder, but Adams couldn't tell if he was referring to the ranch or the dinner they'd just shared.

"You took a good poke at him, aiming the conversation toward women and Charlotte like that. That was a risk I don't appreciate."

"And you stepped right in like the protector you are, didn't you? You've even made sure he's had a chance to charm a new lady friend, that Sugar he talks about. I almost envy the man his fresh opportunities. But you don't need to worry. I heard enough to convince myself that he hasn't really spoken to Charlotte. I don't ca—"

Adams interrupted. "I want some money."

Buren slid his fingers under the flap of a tweed pocket, looking for cigarettes that weren't there. He claimed he'd stopped smoking on President's Day. "Don't we all. Are you asking for my share of the property taxes? Early?"

"You need to listen to me," Adams said. "I want serious money, like a loan without the bank slowdown and bullshit."

"For what? You've already transformed the house into Ye Olde Comfort Home for Aged Gentlemen. I thought the plan was to put up your feet, admire the blank views."

"Sheep," Adams said, getting irritated. "I've given it a lot of thought since C.D. told me about seeing Charlotte. Maybe I was thinking about it even before then, I don't know. But this ranch needs stock. I need stock. I got some help now. It's time for me and the Trumpet Bell to get back into business."

Buren shut his eyes for one extended moment. Adams found himself staring at the skin of his brother's eyelids, which was slack and veined. Then Buren coughed into a phlegmy, knowing laugh, and he kept laughing for a long time as if the sound moving up and down his throat was a better drink than whisky. Adams cursed himself for rushing into his request. He should have gone slow and laid the groundwork. Instead, he'd given his brother a big chance to consider him ridiculous.

"Bless you for . . . for your thick-skinned innocence, Fremont. You maintain it well. I was sure you wanted me to orchestrate a way to pry C.D. out of here, but no, you have positive ideas. You still think you're a landowner with chattel you can organize around you. You still think you've got some sort of family." The cheerful scorn humiliated Adams who hadn't realized until that very moment how much he really wanted the cash for a small herd of sheep and everything it might give him. "*Money—the sinew of love as well as war.* Is this supposed to salve my conscience about what happened with the dynamite and all the rest?"

Adams didn't answer. His hands were laced tight around the polished wood of the broom handle.

"Our dear, departed uncle Gene Laury would cut your tendons like a fatted wether for such impulsive planning. Your fiscal track record is lousy. There's not a bank in the Rockies that would lend you a thin dime."

Adams tried not to look away.

"Money is the only thing I've ever had that you didn't." Buren dropped his voice until its pitch was slow and savage. The phlegm and humor were gone. "You got the ranch and the man-sized character that supposedly goes with it because most of the Stetson heads out here believe that one is absolutely linked to the other. You got the courage because courage is what our mother insisted it took for you to handle Korea, though I suspect you haven't handled a thing about it. You got the love and devotion of our sister, and you treated her like scum, but who could blame you for that, she is an Adams, after all—a person a little too unfettered. You got the community respect, the halo of managing water rights, and you fiddled while Rome went dry because you never learned how to look beyond your own nose. Now, what you ought to do is step aside and let C.D.'s crooked nature run its course. But you can't do it. You *won't*. So, yes. I'm a lifelong student of tragedy. I'll pay to see the final act."

He kicked the snow off the toes of his wingtips as if it was the worst sort of dust. "Is ten thousand dollars enough for me to throw into the winter wind? It's worth it to me—every penny—just to have you suggest that one of us believes in something beyond the purgatory of this place where we grew up." Something like a chuckle came back into Buren's mouth. "Grew up. That's the wrong phrase for the Adams legacy. We have grown nothing. I suspect it's a proper blessing that neither of us ever had children."

He went straight to the barn. Buren, for all his manners and calculation, was a sack of pure shit. It took a while to clean up after a talk with Buren. He had asked his brother for one thing—it wasn't like he'd gone to his knees in desperation—but Buren had still gotten his claws in. He had promised to transfer the money to Adams's bank account even though, he said, they both knew money wasn't really what Adams needed.

The horses were in their stalls, each covered with a quilted blanket. The sorrel was off her feet when Adams came in, but the old roan was awake and alert. He swung his whitened head over his stall door and waited, drawing long breaths through his nostrils. The roan's eyes weren't good, but he knew Adams as soon as he smelled him. The smell made him lift his head higher. Adams went into the tack room, moving through the dark by touch, and he took the heavy lid off the feed barrel and scooped up a measure of feed. He gave each horse a half scoop and stood between their narrow, straw-bedded stalls to listen to them eat. The sorrel stood up and downed the molasses-rinsed grain and cracked corn as fast as she could. She wasn't an animal who savored much. The roan, who was older, and a descendant of fine Texas horses, ate slowly. The noises of his pleasure took some of the heat out of Adams's frustrations. Horses were direct. He'd always liked that about them. The ones he'd loved the most, like the dun colt Jackson he'd trained with the dedication of a master sergeant after his return from Korea, were the ones that were the most predictable.

He could use some of that predictability right now.

Buren was wrong. There wasn't a tin roof nailed over the top of his life. Hell yes, he was sixty-four years old and some-what bad in the back and constantly plagued by arthritis in the feet he'd frozen in Korea. And there were other weaknesses,

like how his belly was bulldogging the steak and scotch he'd
had for dinner. Things didn't go down easy like they once
had. But whatever future he had was still going to be a future
he chose—not one that C.D. Hobbs or Buren chose for him.
The rest of his days weren't going to be about sniffing the thin
smoke of a purpose he'd given up somewhere along the line.
He was going to put sheep back in his corrals. They might be
merinos, the delicate boutique kind of animal he used to laugh
about, but they would still be sheep. He understood their limits. He should never have given up on sheep in the first place.
They were the only safe thing he had ever wanted.

He opened the barn door and slipped into the cocoon of
snow and darkness. Hobbs was cleaning up after their meal.
Adams could see his jerky, deliberate movements through the
yellow square of the kitchen window. He looked like he was
swatting flies. Hobbs's dishwashing was generally all puddles
and chipped plates, but it got the job done. He had enjoyed
the dinner with Buren. He would, Adams knew, enjoy the news
about the sheep even more. So why wasn't he hustling into the
house to share their good fortune? Why did he feel more comfortable in his silence and isolation? The machine shed, large
and white-capped and dented, suddenly seemed more inviting.

He pried at the shed's roll doors with trembling fingers.
He'd come outside with Buren without putting on gloves or a
coat, but he hadn't felt the arrows of winter until now. The
chill spiked into his kidneys. The shed did not feel deserted,
even though he knew Hobbs was still in the house. The air he
eased into his lungs was dense and strangely dry, the kind of air
he associated with packed linens. Slowly, cautiously, he worked
his way from the shed door to Hobbs's workbench in nearly
total darkness. He smelled the clumped grease and mud of his
tractors. He tasted the sour hone of iron and steel. He moved
in silence, believing the silence was in honor of Hobbs and the
work he did in that place. Yet he didn't hesitate to take the
thing he wanted. He made his claim. She was in a lidless green
coffee can, one he'd seen Hobbs wash and polish with a torn
clump of bath towel. Charlotte in miniature—alone in a dry

cistern of memory. He grasped her gently with his thumb and finger; she was the size of a three-inch bolt. The rim of the coffee can was decorated with small shreds of cloth he recognized all too well. He'd seen them on the plundered hills near Chosin. Flags for the dead. Prayers for the spirits of the lost. He swaddled the tiny Charlotte with his right hand. Hobbs might not even miss her. The workbench currently imprisoned a dozen more exactly like her.

The ranch yard was an estuary of snow. He churned across its quiet surface, bisecting the ribbons left by Buren's spinning car tires. He saw no sign of Hobbs or the dogs. The house, which was warm with the scents of beef fat and detergent, seemed empty. He called for Hobbs once, then walked through the kitchen and parlor, flipping off light switches before he ascended the steep cordon of stairs, which creaked as they had creaked for sixty-four years. He went down the hall to the door of Charlotte's room and opened it.

The room was cold because he kept it closed off to save money. A sliver of him expected to see Hobbs there, curled on the mattress with his dogs, though he couldn't say why he expected that. Winter kept the room smelling fresh, the way the root cellar under the house smelled fresh when it was empty. He turned on the light. The space was still entirely Charlotte's. The ivory-colored bureau. The clover-pink walls that matched the dust ruffle on the bed. The dozens of faded 4-H ribbons—reds and purples and greens and yellows—that hung on a clothesline strung above the bed. There was the Viennese music box that had belonged to their mother's mother. And the family pictures tucked along the edges of a mirror frame. Rows of porcelain horses, their legs cracked from rough play, stood on a pair of painted shelves mounted on one wall. The sateen comforter on the bed looked cheap and faded beneath the illumination of the single lightbulb screwed into the ceiling, but it was all hers, maintained as if she'd died as a child.

The figurine had grown warm in the clutch of his hand. It wasn't easy to see her against his skin: Hobbs's princess in a coffee-can tower. His sister as amulet. He thought of her walking the slushy spring streets of Denver, having an entire life he knew nothing about among the brick warehouses and glass towers of the city. He thought about how she wasn't a school-teacher anymore, and he wondered what her eyes looked like. Her sculpted shape was subtle and smooth, as easy to palm as a worn river stone. He touched her head once with the tip of his left thumb. Then he laid her on top of the ivory-painted bureau. There. Hobbs was wrong. They hadn't lost all of Charlotte. Part of her was here and would always be here. He had never let that part go.

He wouldn't try to call her again. Calling would do no good. He'd leave her to a kind of peace in Denver. *You're afraid of love, of everything that matters.* He turned off the light and went to the north window that faced Bell Butte. He parted the heavy curtains and breathed the unsettling of their dust. A fine gauze of falling snow obscured his view of the butte, but he could see the heavy black scrawl of his fence lines running away from the house. Demarcation. That's what he'd always been about, and it had cost him. *You hate everything that's different from you.* He didn't. Not really. He had tried to accept things that were awkward and different into his life. But he was cautious, and he'd too often been slow to act. The result was a man as taut and insubstantial as his fences.

He left the curtains parted, allowing the phosphorus light of winter to probe his sister's room, then he closed the door and crossed the hall to the cluttered, carpeted square where he slept when sleep could find him. Rain was there for the first time in weeks, stretched across the pad of yellow foam that was his bed. Hobbs must have carried him up the stairs. The dog raised his head blindly, his nose working to take in Adams's scent before he lowered his jaw onto his forelegs and closed his eyes once again. Adams said a word for the dog, but he didn't lean over to caress him. He waited, instead, for the sounds of the house to settle over them. How often had he stood in that chipped doorway waiting for his sister to hustle her ass out of the bathroom while they were both getting ready for school? Charlotte had taken plenty of his time in those days, hadn't she? And plenty of his space. He could almost hear it now, the rustle of her importance, her haste, as she passed him in that narrow pioneer hall. Her presence came back to him in a sweet, rising cloud of girl soap and the twin intake of their breaths. They had slipped by each other often in those days, brother and sister. Quickly. Passing familiarly and without touch.

He slept later than he should have, grinding a long dream about Charlotte and her horse, Redrock, between his teeth. Redrock had finally died of old age in the early 1980s. But in his dream the horse had crippled himself while racing at full gallop under the prick of Charlotte's spurs. Redrock jammed a foreleg into a gopher hole, broke it, and fell. But Charlotte did not fall with him, not in the dream. Charlotte rose upward on the pink carpet of her own dust, still spurring, as if she were a thick-husked seed in the wind.

Hobbs was not in the kitchen. There was no breakfast, no coffee, only a greasy plate of leftover mushrooms from the night before. Seven o'clock. Adams could not remember the last time he'd stayed in bed so late. And the sleep hadn't come from whisky, either. It had come from an exhaustion beyond his bones.

He found Hobbs in the shed. But Hobbs wasn't adding new members to his circus; he was hammering at some freshly sawn lengths of 2 x 4, instead. His boots were sprinkled with wood shavings. They resembled a pair of decorated rye cakes.

"What you're making there looks like a piece of feeder gate." Adams rubbed his eyes with the back of a hand. Sawdust always made him itchy.

"S-smart," Hobbs said. "I thought it's what y-you'd want. We need to spruce up them corrals."

"We do, do we?" Adams felt a drill bit of apprehension bore into his ribs.

"Y-yes. For the sheep. The new ones. I was guessing you'd go for yearlings, but I wasn't sure how many. Buren d-didn't say nothing to me. I just. . . ." Hobbs paused, the hammer dangling from his good hand, a pleased dimple to his smile. "I just knew how it should go, Fremont. You've always been a good boss, e-easy to figure, easy to read."

"That so? You enjoy Buren's visit that much?"

Hobbs hung the hammer from his belt. "Buren is like a single note of music to m-m-me. I don't . . . I'd rather not explain how it works when it comes to Buren. He was nice last night. It's nicer that you're buying sheep."

Adams rubbed at his eyes again. He wished he was able to keep himself prepared for Hobbs's surprises. "And how can you tell that without talking to me or looking in a crystal ball, one or the other?"

Hobbs rubbed a fond thumb along the red welt of his recent injury. "It's wrote like a book on your f-face, Fremont. And it's pretty much made a kind of light all around you, just the thoughts you been h-having. It's a thing I learned to see, th-that kind of light."

"Jesus." Adams held back an onrushing sneeze. "You got me, C.D. You're way ahead of me again. You're always ahead of me." He told himself that Hobbs's strangeness was only as strange as he allowed it be. "I reckon I better retire and give up right now."

"N-no," Hobbs said, pulling a handful of nails from somewhere inside his jeans. "That can't be said about you on good days or bad, Fremont. It's what there is to like about you. You're one who never gives up."

The sheep arrived in a welter of bleating and mud, whether they were ready for them or not. The driver of the tri-level stayed long enough to have a cigarette while Adams studied the invoices. Fifty ewes: all registered, all puny. Their shorn flanks heaved above their frail black legs, and their slit eyes—which looked goaty to Adams—were dull with exhaustion. The bucks, which he and Hobbs chuted into the horse pen for close inspection, were worse. There were only two of them. The ewes had already been bred, they didn't even need the bucks, but here they were fat and slack and awkward in their long, untended bodies. The bucks' curled horns were pitted from poor nutrition. "I hate to give them up, but my youngest son's gone for the computers in Seattle." That's what the east Oregon farmer had said. He had made Adams sit through the story of his family's rise and fall in the highlands above the Owyhee River. It was a good story, inflated by improbable luck and honest partnerships that never disappointed. Adams was familiar with it, chapter and verse. It was the ballad a man had to sing when he was left with nothing but overgrazed land and dogs.

Adams told the farmer he'd gotten moldy in retirement and wanted the company of some breeding stock. When the farmer responded with a diatribe against hippies and organic apple orchards in a voice that whistled through its consonants, Adams knew the farmer believed he had the kind of money and leisure time the farmer had only dreamed about. He tried, and failed, to cut off the farmer as the man recited, by tag number, exactly how each ewe liked to be handled before she dropped her lambs. Hearing the farmer evaporate his ranching history into a loose skein of words made Adams's skin pucker.

The ewes were mostly quiet until Hobbs drove the tractor and a wagon filled with seed cake into the front field. Adams closed the gate behind Hobbs and hefted an axe onto his shoulder. As he trailed the tractor, the stunned ewes began to rally and trail it, too. At first, they moved alone or in small groups linked jaw to flank to jaw. They didn't stop to nibble at the clumps of bunchgrass as the spring sun spread like water across their backs. They stumbled directly toward the feed troughs, the one destination they recognized. A few plaintive bleats gathered and harmonized above the shallow contours of the field, and Adams listened to the sound blend with the local uproar of his magpies. He saw the more vigorous ewes butt the submissive ones aside as Hobbs began to shovel feed. While Adams watched, a luscious, unreined panic lunged through him. There was so much for them to do: feed, doctor, tag, brand, record weights and births. He had spent Buren's money as lavishly as a first-time bride. And now he had the chance to know the animals again. Which were boss and which were rogue and which too stupid to make good decisions on the open range. It felt so right, so deeply familiar. A new purpose was within his grasp, and its momentum came from the loud, begging, needful cries of these sheep. Those cries had once stapled his days to his nights as tightly as a saddle tree was stapled to its leathers.

He made his way to the troughs, loosening the scarf he'd wrapped around his throat and feeling his fingers warm to a sweat inside his gloves. Long, layered terraces of cloud marbled the field with shadows that swirled across the banks of Muddy Creek. He saw Rain circle a portion of the herd, the black mask of the dog's face raised as he, too, memorized the possibilities before him. The small band of dark-legged ewes flowed around the feed wagon as balanced and heedless as a flood. Their underfed shanks were still blotched with the purple paint of their Owyhee River brands. The day those brands were replaced with the $\triangle$ of the Trumpet Bell would be a fine day.

"They don't look like m-much," Hobbs said. He was smiling. He had been a smiler ever since they'd first talked about the sheep.

"They never do," Adams said. "Cows make a man feel richer."

Hobbs thrust his shovel into the dusty bank of seed cake and hauled. "Cows make their own kind of trouble. I'm glad you and Buren didn't go for cows."

"Should I ask what would've happened if we had?" Adams gripped the axe so he could lay into the thick ice that covered the watering trough.

"N-no lambs," Hobbs said. "Calves ain't the same, and I'm not ready to take you through a spring season without lambs."

Adams laughed. Then he thought about what Hobbs had really said. "You think this wormy bunch can do the trick?"

He heard Hobbs and his shovel pause, so he raised the axe and broke through the ice in the trough with one swing. The blow soaked his arms and chest with water. After he pulled off his gloves, he began to fish sour chunks of ice from the trough and throw them to the ground.

"We'll l-lose a few," Hobbs said, finally, and Adams knew he was assessing the ewes as he stood on the wagon, looking at their eyes and bellies. He was good at that. He always had been. "Enough'll make it. For what we want."

"And what's that?" Adams asked, his hips and back hot from working. He'd been making a list in his head of all the familiar things he and Hobbs would get to do once the sheep were fed. "I know you like good animals, but what, exactly, do you think we want? Since you're talking about it."

Hobbs peered down at him, then up into the sky that seemed too huge for the one small sun it held. He pushed his orange hunting cap off his sweat-slick head. They hadn't spoken seriously about anything but sheep since Buren's visit. "You remember that fellow B-big Mike from up around Billings, used to herd some for your uncle Gene?"

Adams thought he could conjure up an attitude, if not a face, to go with that name. The Trumpet Bell had seen dozens of men come and go. Big Mike, as he recalled, had been some sort of distant cousin to Old Etchepare. "I believe so. A little."

"Big Mike weren't no good with sheep, or horses n-neither, but he did tell me this story about a wolf that hunted this territory long ago. I believe he w-wanted to scare me. He thought I was the kind who could be scared."

Adams plunged both hands into the slushy water of the trough. He scooped ice onto the ground as noisily as he could. Hobbs hadn't tried to tell him a story of this kind in quite a while. The warning buzz in his head suggested he should pay attention to the details of this one.

"There was this wolf, see, a big lone male that come down from Montana before the ranchers were all in here. He ate all the b-buffalo he could get. He ate all the elk. It got so the Crow people and the Sioux was afraid of him and glad when he left their country. Big Mike said it was a giant wolf and bright as silver by the time it got to the Ferris Mountains because of all the miners it had swallowed for its meals. That wolf glowed with the glow of their riches. I don't remember all the parts of how he told it. Big Mike was mean and unfriendly in his speaking, s-so if you don't remember him, I'm glad you don't. The ending had to do with a Indian girl who lived along a deep stretch of the Platte River. She somehow fooled that wolf into drowning himself in that water, she saved herself with some kind of special trick, and that's why they say the Platte Canyon runs so pretty and silver in the spring."

Adams wagged his head, wanting Hobbs to see he was amused. "I'm glad to say those damn dogs the government plans to restock in Yellowstone Park will never be allowed to get down this far again. Wolves won't bother us. They are one thing us hard-working sheep men don't have to worry about."

"Th-that's not why I'm saying what I'm saying, Fremont."

Adams glanced upward again. Some of the bolder ewes were butting at his knees now, thirsty for a drink. There were sheep scratching their backs against the wagon axles and tires. He could smell the dispensing scent of their long, desperate journey from Oregon, the piss and shit of animals that have been trapped. "Then why'd you bring it up?"

"I don't know for sure. They just come out of my mouth sometimes, the s-stories. They make these shapes in my m-mind. You're the man who likes a goal he can see and touch."

Adams shook his head. A strange, hard pressure in his skull made it seem as though his ears were about to pop. "What's that mean? That mean you got a prediction, some kind of sensation, about a big wolf bearing down on us now that we got something to protect?"

"N-no," said Hobbs, closing his eyes. "It ain't that complicated. It's not about seeing one danger, or even two. Danger's always there. Y-you can't get rid of it. She says it's about living with what makes you happy until the day you die."

Adams didn't have to ask who she was. He felt a clutching at his spine, as if distant fingers were digging toward his heart. "Jesus, C.D. I don't know how you manage to make all these connections, but you do. Is it all right if we don't talk about my sister? I can't do Charlotte right now, I really can't. This is a big day for me—for us. I'd rather talk about wolves and these brand-new merinos. I might still have a chance to get things right with them."

Hobbs drove his shovel into the load of seed cake. He lifted a bladeful and added it to the trough, careful not to dump it on the desperate heads of the ewes. "See, that's your story, Fremont. And you tell it p-pretty good. I like it. These merino gals like it. You got c-confidence. The confidence has come back. You don't give away no sense of how there might some day be a finish to things. Y-you don't go for the end. That's what you leave for everybody else, ain't it? H-how it all ends."

"You keep him away from me, that's what you need to do. Right now."

Adams unclamped his teeth, thinking that might improve his hearing. His wristwatch said it was one in the morning. The television was a cold beacon beyond his feet. He'd fallen asleep in his recliner, or that's what the magazine on his lap seemed to indicate. He was holding the receiver of the phone to his ear, though he didn't remember picking it up.

"He's been up here twice this week, and friends of mine saw him at the bar in Sinclair. Maybe you don't know that. Maybe you think it's not your beeswax." The voice was female, fast and toothy. He didn't . . . he couldn't think who it might be. He remembered eating calf liver and onions for dinner. He could taste those on his breath. And there had been some sort of dream, a physical pursuit that was hungry and troubling. He hadn't slept well since he'd gotten the merinos. Grogginess still had him nailed flat.

"Wake up," the voice shrieked. "I ain't kidding. He's following me all over the place and it's getting outta hand. There's them'll do something if you won't. It don't matter how brave he thinks he is. How he thinks there's something to hisself when he drinks."

Hobbs? Was she talking . . . could it be Sugar? Was it Sugar on the phone? He tried to unkink his neck to see if the Ford truck was in the yard, but he was laid out stiff in the recliner, couldn't see a damn thing from there.

"He. . . . Is this . . . jail?" It was all he could put together on short notice. The woman and her voice were way ahead of him.

"No, this ain't no jail or snitch. This is a Good God Damn Citizen telling you somebody you should be taking care of is off the rails." She paused to suck in some breath, and Adams decided she was no drunker than he was. She didn't breathe like a drunk. "Tell him what I said. Tell him to leave me the hell alone." And she hung up.

He held onto the phone long after he needed to. It kept talking at him—errrrr, errrrr, errrrr. He rubbed his face and stared at the haft of moonlight that stood guard between the imperfectly closed window curtains and tried to assemble what he knew. It was April. Close to lambing time. There were inoculations to give. Bills to pay. He'd sent Hobbs to the bank in Rawlins that afternoon, but Hobbs had been back by sundown. They'd been together every day since the sheep arrived, utterly busy except at night, and who knew how either of them made it through one of those.

Could Hobbs be tomcatting at night?

Tell him. . . . Tell him. . . . This was a new responsibility. It had been decades since he'd had to protect C.D. Hobbs from anybody outside his own family. He didn't know what he was supposed to say, how something like this got addressed. But address it he would. He rubbed the distant mask of his face again, then studied the dissolved edges of the room and all its furniture. He knew what the room would tell him. The room would tell him what it had told him before: he had to take care of C.D. Hobbs. Without Hobbs, this was it right here, all there ever was day after day after day—a box and him inside it.

He fed the horses well before dawn, then turned them out into the hoof-chewed paddock that smelled of frost and stone. He could just make out the shape of Bell Butte as it rose above the roofline of the house. It looked like a black-handled reef awash in the light of the fading stars. He made himself go into the machine shed, and he made himself knock on Hobbs's door. There was no answer. When he pushed open the door, the dogs Zeke and Dan unfurled themselves from the camp bed and came to nudge at his boots. There was no sign of Hobbs, or Rain, although the Mexican blanket on the bed had been carefully folded across the foot of Hobbs's sleeping bag. The harder part came when he discovered that the old flatbed International that had once been their ditching truck was no longer parked on the east side of the barn.

So, that was it. Hobbs had gone off into the night after Sugar and her friends, whether he was welcome or not. The knowledge of Hobbs's capering and drinking dried itself like rawhide around his gullet and jaw.

He wasn't given much time to suffer in his worries. He took his shepherd's crook and the two ignorant dogs and moved into the cold cave of the day, hoping that motion, a walk to survey his modest holdings, would ease his thoughts. The pasture that held the merinos was still white with a few crusts of snow, but it didn't take him long to see the dead ewe for what she was. Her body was pressed against a stretch of woven-wire fence. Her belly was bloated, and her tongue was thick and gray between her lips. Her hooves had cut sharp crescents in the ground as they spasmed. There was no blood, so Adams knew she hadn't been taken down by coyotes. It was likely she'd gone septic from a dead lamb. Her loss was unfortunate, but not unusual. That was how he was thinking before he found the second one.

She was on a slope east of the feed troughs. She wasn't bloated. Instead, she appeared desiccated, her hide furrowed with signs of dehydration. Birds had eaten at her upward facing eye while she was still alive, leaving ants a hole into the ripe skull beneath. Adams glanced overhead for the soaring scrap of a raven, then back at a carcass the dogs wouldn't even sniff. The remaining ewes seemed unperturbed. They migrated into the golden bays of sunlight that began to pool across his mottled field, grazing with their usual single-minded efficiency. Adams put his fingers to his mouth and whistled. When he had both dogs at his feet, he had to keep himself from etching the hour and the date in his calamitous memory. For more than two weeks, he and Hobbs had had a ranch operation that was right and lucky. He was not ready to mark this moment as the beginning of its inevitable demise. He just wasn't.

He cast the dogs in wide, sweeping arcs and limped his way to the gate that led toward the corrals. He pressed his feet hard against the rolls of flannel he used to fill out the ends of his boots where he no longer had toes. He would need all of his quickness, all of his balance, to pen the herd on his own. But he could do it. He had done it before many, many times, even in storms that left him deaf and blind. As the ewes began to bellow and bunch and turn in response to the prodding of the dogs, he unlatched the field gate and let it swing wide. He gripped his crook in both hands. The morning wind swept toward him, and into him, from the mallow crest of Powder Rim, and he let the wind fill him like a sail. He closed his eyes so hard he could feel his pulse thrum against their lids. He could do it again, he could, he could. He needed no soul other than his own, no friend, no partner, to work this perfect thing.

But the dogs had been unevenly trained, and the merinos didn't yet know the layout of his ranch. They came at the gate like they didn't see it. Zeke moved off the heels of a lagging ewe and thrust himself in front of her, nipping at her tender chin. This corked the movement of the herd, so Adams waded into the confusion with his crook held high. He shouted encouragement, he cajoled, he spooked Zeke back into position with a swing of his crook, and it all worked well enough until he tried to high-step free of the chaos. He'd just hooked the haunch of a blundering ewe from behind when he fell. And though she wasn't big enough to drag him, she was strong enough, and frightened enough, to yank hard on his shoulder. The tear went through his right side like the tearing of fine cloth. The pain came right after.

He lay on the ground as his livestock bucked and farted its way past his aching head. The dogs were good enough to finish the job he had started; they pressed all forty-eight remaining ewes into the corral. He got to his feet, careful to pin his arm against his side as if it were a broken wing. He latched the gate with his left hand. In better days, younger days, he would have been ready to joke about his clumsiness, if not his frailty. He'd been hurt plenty of times. But he could find no joke in his spinning mind. A real rancher never minded when his stock got the better of him—not as long as it only happened once in a while. All right, he told himself, you are a real rancher. This is not for pretend. Nothing that really matters has gotten the jump on you.

He hung onto the swaying gate for a moment, catching his breath. He watched the black blade of a scavenging raven slice across the carnation petals of a high-flying cloud. It was headed for his dead ewes, damn bird. It hadn't been slowed down or undermined by its instincts. It knew what job it was supposed to do. And so did he.

Once he'd swallowed some of his embarrassment, Adams examined the gathered herd and decided that some of his merinos looked good and some appeared as dazed and starved as the day they had shipped in. The fine spice-colored dust of the corrals clumped at their tear ducts and nostrils, making them all seem weepy, but he tried to make distinctions. He tried to think through the most pressing problem he had—the death of the ewes. Was there poisonweed in the pasture or some kind of fungus in the seed cake? Had the sheep carried in a bug from Oregon? He had so many questions—and no one to ask them to. Where the hell was Hobbs? Why would he stay away in the morning? He spent a short, throbbing moment appraising the two bucks that had roused themselves in response to the arrival of the ewes. Both had forage-green slobber matted on their muzzles and chests, and their blatting calls wavered with uncertainty. What ugly luxuries they were. They had no good reason to be in the world.

Hoping the situation might be one that had a simple solution, Adams gimped his way into the dry vacancy of the machine shed.

"C.D.," he shouted. "I god damn need you, you know. I need you right now." His voice roused only the sparrows that nested in the building's eaves. They fled from his echoing voice like a handful of hurled stones.

The veterinarian was new to Baggs, one in a long line of doctors who served the area on rotation and never stayed for long. But she knew her sheep, and she was smart enough not to make promises. She took samples from the two bodies Adams had kicked onto the front loader of the big tractor and left elevated, like a raised dish of meat, in the ranch yard. She helped the injured Adams chute a pair of healthy-looking ewes so she could collect their blood and urine. She didn't seem convinced the deaths were caused by a single ailment, some kind of epidemic barreling down on him out of nowhere.

"I've read. . . ." The new vet paused, dampening her student impulse. "A Colorado fellow told me it's hard for some breeds to adapt to the harsh conditions up here. Have you raised merinos for long?"

"Sixty-nine years," he blurted. Then he had to correct himself and repeat the brief history of the Trumpet Bell he'd given her when she arrived. "It's my first shot at merinos, I admit that. I can't see what Colorado has to do with anything." He knew he sounded like a maidenish old man who hadn't eaten breakfast and who'd just had his shoulder torn loose, but god damn it, he respected the fact this child vet had gone to school way over at Iowa State, she ought to respect him.

Hobbs finally showed up behind the wheel of the backfiring International truck just before the vet departed. He was wearing a brand-new hat and shirt. He had another necklace around his neck. This one looked like it had started its life as a bicycle chain. The vet went over her assessment again, for Hobbs's benefit—what they should watch for and how some culling, followed by injections of medicine they could get from her office might be their best option. Hobbs didn't ask any questions. He suspended his wide mouth in an open, fluted shape while the doctor spoke. Adams stared at Hobbs, trying to smell liquor on him or at least the sweat of late-night dancing and its aftermaths, but he couldn't detect what he wanted to detect—hints of guilt or ruin. Hobbs also didn't seem particularly upset about the dead ewes. He was polite to the vet, cautious with Adams, but he appeared oddly calm.

"She's nice," Hobbs said as they watched the vet's customized Dodge fishtail onto the highway.

"For what she's selling, sure. Nice and smart and expensive as all get out. How's the ditch truck run?" It was Adams's way of asking Hobbs where the hell he had been all night. He did it with a shaved voice.

"Stops every few miles. Thirsty as a c-camel for water. Oil, too." Hobbs squatted to look at the two lolling bucks through the warped slats of the horse pen.

"This herd doesn't have to be a job for both of us," Adams said, "in case you've got more important things to do."

Hobbs answered with words as flat as the ground they stood on. "Nothing's more important."

"Then why is the telephone waking me up at night, filling my ears with news of your adventures? I can see how the partying might be fun for you, but I thought we'd agreed on something here. We got a business to run."

"We have b-business," Hobbs muttered, squinting at the dirty, placid bucks. "We have business. We have business."

Adams felt the blood rush to his face. "Could you at least stay home at night? I don't want somebody to hurt . . . I worry that . . . Jesus, I just want to say that I could use your help and attention with this sick bunch of ewes."

Hobbs removed the new, unhandled straw hat from his head. His eyes were like split shot. "You don't look so good this morning, F-fremont. You're hearing all this news as bad. Has anybody ever t-told you that you see too many things as s-sick or bad? These sheep ain't sick. I wouldn't let them bring you any kind of disease."

"What are you—" Adams stopped and held his breath hot behind his teeth. Listening to this version of Hobbs talk was like listening to somebody read from a torn and plundered book. Too many pages were missing. Too much failed to make sense.

"The t-t-telephone's not about me," Hobbs continued. "I don't know what you mean by that. Where I go is not a place that's got t-telephones. I can't g-go very fast in that truck, but there's a lot to see when I get up toward the sky. G-galaxies, p-planets, all that sort of thing. Th-there's lots of nice parts in the sky a person can see if he knows how to ask."

"Would you please—" But Adams couldn't continue the scolding. Hobbs was obviously lying to him. He'd been gone the same time somebody was stalking Sugar. There had to be a connection. And the way he talked. Planets? Galaxies? Christ almighty, maybe there was just no hope. Maybe insanity was as inevitable as the arrival of summer. Adams dropped his eyes. He didn't want Hobbs to see the belief that was fracturing inside him.

"Don't w-worry, Fremont." Hobbs stood, serenading Adams with his hingeless smile. "You look so worried. It'll happen like it h-has to happen. You're running sheep like you love to do, and you're mad I wasn't here. Y-you're telling me you need more help. All right. I c-can fix that. I got a idea for that."

Hobbs sauntered long-legged into the machine shed and soon sauntered out again. He held a black barrel lid in front of himself like a tray, and he began to circle the sheep corrals, pausing every few feet to touch the low wooden fences with his fingers. The sullen ewes barely reacted to his presence, but the young dogs yipped and whined and leaped at Hobbs's flashing hands. He progressed deliberately, like a man laying out survey stakes. Adams knew what it all meant even before Hobbs ducked back into the machine shed to resupply. Hobbs was bringing his little friends out to play. He was setting them up as guards around their indefensible world.

Adams moved closer to the fence and grabbed one of the figures. It was a marine, barefoot, unarmed, distinguished by a face that was all eyes. It was all he could do not to hurl the figure to the ground. Oh, he'd been a damn fool to believe in normal deeds like tractor repair and kitchen floors and merinos. He dug the rough points of his fingernails into his callused palms. Normal never won out at the Trumpet Bell. There was no such thing as an undisturbed, healing life on his ranch—and he was no healer. There was truly nothing left of his home place except its name and its ability to skin men out like pelts.

Hobbs gamboled his way up the loading chute, the young dogs on his heels. Rain, meanwhile, curled himself into a dark comma at Adams's feet. Adams watched Hobbs drive one of his larger figurines into the soft wood of the chute with the heel of his hand as if he were driving a nail. He felt each blow in the floor of his belly. He watched Hobbs hang what looked like a strand of shiny beads around the figurine's tiny neck. "You don't got to w-worry, Fremont. We all need a little more help from t-time to time." Hobbs plucked two more shapes from his barrel lid and slipped them into his shirt pocket as a pair. Adams tried to see who made up the pair: himself and Hobbs, Charlotte and Hobbs, Devlin and Hobbs. Each possibility riddled him with a different brand of guilt. He set the silvery, barefoot marine back on its fence post, its pained eyes aimed toward the setting sun. Hobbs balanced himself on the front edge of the loading chute and began to flap his old-man arms as if they were feathered wings. "It's good, ain't it, Fremont? Th-this is how it gathers. Things won't be like they used to be. This is all the h-h-help we'll ever need."

"Been awhile," the voice said. "I don't get down there no more. It don't feel right to come even when I miss it like a missing leg."

"Steve?" he asked. "Steve Barnheisel?" Adams hadn't wanted to answer the phone. He had let it ring itself out twice because Hobbs was gone again, had been gone since he'd cleared off his workbench, so Adams believed the phone could only bring him bad news. Plus, his shoulder hurt like hell whenever he reached for anything. Then he'd gotten mad at himself for being afraid of what the phone might tell him. Jesus god, he was tougher than that, hurt shoulder or no hurt shoulder. He'd lost another ewe that afternoon and had burned her where she died, watching her smoke like an untended skillet. His hands still smelled of gasoline. If Hobbs was already on his way to cuckoo, what did he have to be afraid of?

"Yeah, it's me, the old fart who quit on you. Right now I'm living in a house the size of a wool sack. Mexicans to the right of me, Mexicans to the left of me, there's a lot of Mexicans in Casper even when it's winter. How you doing, Fremont?"

"I'm doing." He produced words that rang with the conviction he knew Steve Barnheisel, neighbor and former hand, expected.

"Don't know if you've heard, I guess you haven't or you'd be saying something about it, but Buren is in the hospital up here. He wanted me to let you know."

Adams stopped breathing.

"Buren," Steve repeated. "Your brother? He told me to call."

Adams tried to loosen the tentacles clenched around his spine. "Did he wreck his car?"

"No. You really hadn't heard, have you? I guess it helps that my granddaughter nurses at the medical center, so I'm in that loop. Sammi, she's Trina's girl. Nice kid. It weren't a car accident. He come into the emergency yesterday morning, after midnight. Sammi was on a twelve-hour shift. Police brought Buren in, she says, and he was smashed up bad. He had enough eyesight to read Sammi's name tag, I don't know how that happened but it did. Sammi's got my name just like Trina does because Trina and her boyfriend never managed to get married. Buren made a joke about it, her name—this was when he was still talking—and Sammi put two and two together. So I went up there this morning to see what I could do, we've known each other for so long. Buren wrote your name down on a pad since he can't— Well, hell, he's beat bad. Somebody took it to him."

"How bad?" He made himself say it, thinking all the time about the bones of the burned ewe that lay in a scorched halo on the open page of his field.

"He's gonna make it. I shoulda said that first. I'm not used to being the . . . talking like this isn't what I know how to do.

He's not dying, nothing like that. But he's got the jaws wired, bruises all over his face. Lot a stitches. I think Sammi said one of his knees is about smashed to pudding. In a parking lot near the Safeway is where they found him, and there'd been drinking. They found broke bottles on the pavement. What he writes on paper to the police makes it sound like he don't know what happened to him, but there's been a lawyer to his room, more than one as a matter of fact. Lawyers he knows, I guess. And Sammi says the talk is it was over a woman. I'm not sure I get that. I remember you being a cat for women, not Buren, but there's plenty I don't know, I suppose. He was staying at the Parkway. His car's still there."

"I better make the trip."

Steve Barnheisel made a sluggish cluck with his tongue. "I don't know what to tell you about that, Fremont. A visit's not what he asked for."

Adams waited. He'd stretched the black curlicue of the phone cord as far as it would stretch. He paced his way almost into the kitchen, making the cord twirl from its own tension.

"He wanted to write a message. You know how Buren is, can't make nothing easy. At first I couldn't read half his words. Sammi says he's maybe on more painkillers than he thinks. I kept after it, though. It's like he needs you to finish some list for him. He kept writing your name, then what looks like the word sugar or S-U-G or something. When I said those letters out loud to him, he nodded straight up and down, like that was it. All you needed to know."

"Christ."

"I'll tell him I talked to you, Fremont. And I got a phone number for his hospital room. Then I might just step back on this one, though I hope I'll get to see you if you come up here. That Buren—" Adams could almost smell the rancid truth of Steve's sigh. "That brother of yours, he is not easy to be around."

He thought about it for a long time, longer than it deserved maybe, but the thinking didn't come easy. It was like climbing over wet scree in the rain—you could only get where you were going with a lot of clawing and shifting and sliding. He went out onto the porch where he could see the unchangeable flare of the evening sun—golden, smeared, effortless. Then he went back inside and took the shotgun off the rack and loaded it with slugs he kept in a box on the windowsill in the mudroom. His rifle was gone, another connection he'd failed to make, but the shotgun would do. He could handle it with one hand. He slipped his right elbow into the sling he'd made from a saddle strap and crossed the ranch yard with a simple, sealed-off urgency he hadn't felt in a long time.

Jesus, he'd been stupid, and it was the stupid who were led astray. Like idiot lambs. He had never come close to guessing that it was his lonely son-of-a-bitch brother Buren who was bothering Sugar. Buren must have trailed her to Casper and Sinclair, and maybe other places too, trying to buy her drinks like it was his right to pursue her and upstage C.D. Hobbs whenever he felt like it. It hadn't quite gotten him killed, but it had gotten him busted up enough for police photos and trials and lawsuits, which were precisely the kinds of fun houses Buren understood. Jesus. It was just like his sick, arrogant brother to get exactly what he wanted. He was half dead, and probably more alive than he'd been in years. Now he would have a righteous goal once again. Adams knew Buren would harass Sugar or whoever had done her fighting for her until he had their very last penny and their dreams.

He got to the horse pen and let himself in through the high-swinging pole gate. He shot the first buck where it lay, right in the head, shattering the upper portion of its goaty skull. The second one ran from him. It hit the far end of the pen and tried to climb the slats with its soft, forked hooves. When that failed, the buck began to butt the fence with its thick brow, never turning to look back at the danger, never ceasing its instinctive, absurd movement. Adams watched the humping drive of its shaggy ass, thinking to himself that some things in the world just had to be stopped and ended, then he moved to his left, aimed, and shot the buck behind the shoulder. The shot slapped through rib and meat and the warm, pressured air of the buck's lungs, and the animal was down and finished before the sounds of its death had run their scale. Adams left the bodies where they lay. It was still too cold for flies. And if he shut the gate, which he did, there would be no way in for coyotes.

He returned to the house, made coffee but didn't drink it, cleaned the shotgun with oil and a rag until the throb in his shoulder made his eyes burn. He piled his wood box with more kindling than he would use in a week. He filled several buckets with curled magazines and phone books that he swore he'd drive to the county dump. But nothing brought relief. Even when he realized he wouldn't be able to stop himself, he began to tear down, unhook, and dismantle all the tawdry belongings that he considered his. The parlor floor became tiled with faded, unshelved books, and his father's picture of the Grand Tetons lay bent and flapping behind the cabbage-rose settee. The woodstove roared with the conflagration of burning files and correspondence. When the room looked and felt as abandoned as he did, he put on a coat and hat and gloves and went outside to keep vigil on his porch. He wasn't sure what he was waiting for, what he thought was going to arrive and finish him off for good, but he knew what was leaving him. He could see it lifting and whirling into the sky above his house. The small shreds of his life rose red through a single chimney. They blew across his scattered lands on a slack prairie wind, cooling and crumbling and falling into untraceable smudges of nothing.

He didn't have long to wait. When it was light enough for the hungriest of the magpies to glide into his ranch yard from its cottonwood perch along Muddy Creek, he forced himself to feed the horses and the remaining sheep. He fueled that hapless chore with mutterings of self-hatred and slugs of scotch straight from the bottle. He was inhaling a harsh breakfast of nicotine, trying to decide whether he should murder the handsome bird that had begun to peck at the bodies of the slaughtered bucks, when he heard the distant bark of a dog. It was

Rain, he was sure of it. Rain was calling to him from some-where on the butte.

He whistled for the dog, heard nothing more, then staggered into the house for his binoculars. The sun was a fist of white thorns to the east. He squared himself against the cold clay of the yard and glassed the dawn-tipped ridges of the Trumpet Bell. Before long, the sun winked at him from the fenders of the old International truck. The truck was on a trail at the base of Bell Butte, not a mile from the house. It looked like it had gotten high-centered on some stumps of sagebrush. He did not see Hobbs, but he did spot Rain looking dead-whipped near the rear of the truck. There was also a glint of flat light from the crown of the butte. Maybe he was being glassed, too. He wondered when Hobbs had gotten back to the ranch. Then he wondered whether Hobbs and the dog had ever left at all.

He started after them with the small John Deere, but he left the tractor at the fence line of the alfalfa meadow. If he needed to tow the truck, he could come back for the John Deere. It seemed easier, somehow—though slower—to hoof it straight across the prairie and up the hill. He pulled down the flaps of his hunting cap and checked his pockets for keys and coins he wouldn't need. He had already made up his mind to carry the shotgun.

Zeke and Dan accompanied him in a squall of lunges and casts. They preferred him when they believed he had work to do. They fell away, nevertheless, as he picked a difficult route through the greasewood and wind-glossed snow. To them, loy-alty remained a matter of distance.

The shadows he traversed clawed long and blue toward the west. The rasp of his movements reminded him, as he didn't need to be reminded, of the doomed marine retreat from Chosin Reservoir. Fewer than two thousand men had made it out of Chosin alive, and he was one of them, and for what? For what? Every fourth or fifth step inspired phantom pain from his missing toes. His shoulder ached like a bad tooth. When he crossed the barren wheel ruts of the Overland Trail, a

stretch of stagecoach-carved mud that the federal government
had been pestering him to preserve, he paused to look for the
International. He couldn't see it. He was on the low point of
his land, a washed-out road that people who had never lived
outside a city wanted him to save. No scars on the scars of
history—that was their reasoning. Well, to hell with them. History was nothing *but* scars. He was living proof of that.

He did not have to turn around to know how he felt about
everything that was behind him. The ranch, perhaps, was sal-
vageable. With enough money and optimism, they usually were.
But he was not. He could hear the bleats of his vestigial sheep—
thoughtless and eager—and he knew they had been a bad idea.
Too sentimental. Too impractical. The sheep were the result of
a body that kept waking up alive and its need—or, hell, call it a
desire—to manage animals the way he might have managed all
the better extensions of himself.

He passed the gray kilter of an old docking pen. He crossed
the collapsed bowel of Bell Butte ditch. His feet, as always, finally gave way to the dead Korean cold.

Hobbs wasn't at the truck. Adams called out his name and
got nothing, not even the dog. The truck keys were in the ignition, however. What he was supposed to do seemed clear. He
was supposed to let Hobbs go nuts and clean up afterwards.
He placed the shotgun in the truck bed with a hollow feeling
in his arms and legs. It took him several trips to collect enough
rocks to wedge beneath the truck tires so that the differential
would rise over the sagebrush when he did a fancy dance on
the clutch. When the truck was free, he allowed himself a bitter
smile. Two men could have done the job in less than five minutes. For one man, it was an elegy.

He rolled the truck downhill until he reached a faint track
that shouldered west of the butte. He drove the snowy ruts
carefully, avoiding deep drifts and badger holes. It was the way
he'd driven when his ewes were fat and sleek and ready to
drop loose-skinned lambs, and anticipation was a thing to be
cultivated.

He got out of the truck at a place they called Indian Sink, opened the gate, and drove through. The gate was adjacent to the site for Bell Butte Well #3, a wrecked pad that had gone dry on him and Buren in 1979, a time when failed gambles still led Adams and his raucous neighbors to throw up their ranchers' hands and laugh. There had seemed no end to things in those days. Oil. Gas. Deeds to more acres than you could drive across in a single day. Now there was nothing left of the well but a pair of rust-sutured condensation tanks. If there had ever been much oil, maybe the money would have kept the polish on the Trumpet Bell. His old age, Adams thought, would be banked away in some vault.

He latched the gate at Indian Sink with a loop of wire and gave one more whistle for the dog, Rain. His lips were so dry the sound they made was akin to the hiss of a propane leak. It didn't matter. The dog didn't show. But when he jammed the truck into gear, Hobbs was suddenly there, a flumed shape in his rearview mirror.

Adams was startled. Hobbs had gotten inside his peripheral vision, not an easy thing to do on that broad jut of hill where everything but the junipers was the color of bleached cowhide. He had his thumb primed like a hitchhiker. Adams had seen that pose only once, he'd swear it, and that had been for the benefit of a gnashing, heat-boiled marine sergeant at Camp Pendleton. The sergeant, as everybody knew, had been badly whip-sawed on Guadalcanal. Hobbs was the first, and last, recruit who tried to joke with him.

Adams stood on the clutch, then reached over and opened the passenger door while the truck was still rolling.

"S-sorry about the truck, Fremont. I wasn't driving too good. Whyn't you stop? I want you to s-s-see something." Hobbs was dip-shouldered and grinning. There was a thick smear of something on one cheek, and his doeskin gloves were dark with what looked like axle grease. He kept his eyes on the chromed handle of the truck door, appraising it as if he'd never seen one before. He didn't touch it.

Adams set the brake, but left the truck engine running. That was a joke of his own. It suggested that he and Hobbs would be finished with their encounter in one short minute. Or two.

He got out and faced what was in front of him.

He'd climbed Bell Butte from this direction many times as a boy, they all had, despite his mother's warnings about rattlesnakes and his father's tales of child-eating lions, tales of skulking Ute warriors—so many false tales. When had the butte, that hunch of sandstone and burled light, gone bad on him? He'd shot his share of eagles from its shit-frosted brink, illegally of course, but the damned things had been taking his lambs, and he'd never felt one stab of grief. He had loved the rock's height and permanence. He had admired its stature. Now he could hardly bear to look at the fraudulent mountain that had hovered over his family and their enterprises for two culled-out generations. Bell Butte had finally deserted him as so many things had, everything but Hobbs and memory. Maybe that was how it had to be. It made him like every old man he'd ever known.

He looked into the valley of his empty household and saw vultures corkscrewing the sky above the corrals.

He believed it was his duty to begin the talking. "You up here to earn us a new fortune in oil?"

"No. Uh-uh," Hobbs said. "Though it brings the stink back, don't it? Stink of times g-gone by. I was good on a rig once." He tugged at his cap, a freebie from the hardware store in Rawlins. Its bill was already skeined with grease, maybe graphite. Hobbs's eyes looked strangely white to Adams, as if they were sealed over by an inner distraction.

"I heard some of them at the post talking about the arthritis or bad hearts. C-cancer," Hobbs continued. "How is it that we never talk like that?"

Adams began to relax himself into a shrug, then thought better of it. "Not because we're so different, C.D. We're not. We just haven't got to it yet."

"Think we will?"

"If you want."

Hobbs gaped his wide mouth until his teeth were uncovered. "I like how you believe it's a option, Fremont. You're a b-believer. I remember plinking gophers up here for money from your uncle Gene. You remember that? P-penny for each one. You were always the best shot."

"And Buren the worst."

"Well, sure." Hobbs crowbarred a true laugh from his lungs. "Buren was always the worst."

Adams paused as the wind pressed against the back of his neck, cold and unmannerly. He listened to it toss grit against the pitted windshield of his truck. "I guess you heard me shoot them last evening," he said. "Those damn bucks."

Hobbs nodded. "I worried for a minute you'd shot the horses. Then I decided you wouldn't d-do that. I'm sorry I had the rifle. A rifle's neater."

"It don't matter," Adams said.

"Are more of them sick?"

"Some, probably. I haven't looked this morning. Don't want to. They're a weak bunch, and I haven't handled them so good."

"You handle them fine. I hadn't seen anybody so good at it since Etch and G-Gene. You got the knack." Hobbs's body was so enthusiastic even the binoculars that hung around his neck took on a happy sway. "K-keep on it. You ain't meant to give it up."

"I already have. Starting again was a damn stupid idea. The whole bunch of them has already stomped on me and run me over."

"N-not stupid," Hobbs insisted.

"Well, here's something that is. My brother got himself attached to your friend Sugar. He's caused some serious trouble." He went on to tell how Buren had overstepped himself and landed in the hospital with his jaw wired shut.

Hobbs etched at the dry ground with his steel-toed boots, absorbing the news. His eyebrows drew themselves into a straight line as if he was reworking some kind of internal calculation. Finally, he puckered his mouth and gave a little whistle. He said, "*Death is a punishment to some people, and to others it's a gift.* I b-been practicing how to say that. I taught the words to myself for you and Buren, especially Buren."

"I'm happy to say my brother's not here to ruin our day. What you been memorizing?"

"How to explain. Th-there's a thing I want to explain."

Adams stared at his own feet. "What are you telling me, C.D.?"

"I only saw Sugar that one time in Rawlins. We never did g-get to be real friends, though it would have b-been nice. I just didn't have the time. Anyhow, I'm sorry Buren found trouble, but I have a announcement on the schedule. I-it's time to go."

Adams cupped his hands behind his ears. "Say that again."

"It's time to go."

He began to understand what had been laid out on that trampled well pad, what he had been led there to perceive since that had always been his role, he the scout, Hobbs the one who bore the consequences. This was the balance between them that he'd never tried to change. The well's pump shed had been crudely reassembled—he finally noticed that. He could see tire treads, and boot prints, and deep drag marks leading up to the shed now that he was looking for them. And he knew exactly what was inside that shed. He could visualize how Hobbs would set things up. There would be an overhauled gas generator cross-wired to a waxy packet of dynamite. That way, Hobbs could be sure this explosion was triggered on his terms.

His body came back into itself when he felt heat and stirring near one of his dangled hands. It was his old dog, Rain.

"You got the shotgun with you?" Hobbs's voice was singsong and terrible.

"Yes."

"Want to use it again?"

Adams didn't withhold his answer. He'd done a lot wrong in his life—maybe too much—but he could still call himself honest. "No, I don't."

"Good. That's not the way I have it in my head, just so you know. My h-head doesn't have us struggling over this one." Hobbs defused his eyes, and Adams saw a glimmer of stillness within them, an ocean-rich column of blue. "It's not like any-body t-told me how it has to go, not a preacher or a dream or anything like that. This is *my* answer. I just see the way *I* have to be. It s-seems right after all these scarecrow years."

"I guess . . . I don't know what to say." Adams heard some-thing begin to restore itself in his voice. It came very quickly, a pure gout of letters, and then it was gone. "Do you have to—leave?"

"I ain't left you yet, F-fremont. And I won't ever leave you—not in a way that matters. That house might be empty, but you're not empty. This is what you got to learn. For a long time we've kept each other going on and on. But you've got something to take care of down there." Hobbs pointed a finger toward the toppled dominos of the ranch.

"No. There's nothing left to that."

"There is. Sh-she's gonna come—and you got to be home. She'll come to the graves to see your ma and your father and me."

His mouth wouldn't make the sound he wanted.

"She gave me this to give to you," Hobbs said, as he un-furled a stained and empty hand. He seemed to see something in that hand that Adams did not. He reached out, and Adams reached out, and their bodies touched one last time.

Adams turned to water at the hips and knees. "I d-don't. . . . I just wanted . . . I w-want to help you—"

Hobbs cut him off with a captivated grin. "I thank you for trying. Old Etch would say we stayed wh-who we were and that it was a good thing. What I don't know is how it ends for you. Who's to say what's best for a human man? I never did get a answer to that one." He turned and blinked into the striations of the morning breeze. "B-but this ain't never been about the two of us squawking. Some things don't ever get taken away from people, Fremont. Some things we keep inside us forever," he said. "I n-need you to remember that."

Then he walked in his slow, pronating way toward the shed. It sounded as though he said one last thing to his friend John Fremont Adams, but Adams couldn't be sure of the words.

Wait for her. Don't forget. Your turn. Which was the answer to his question? Uncertainty rooted him to the crumbled soil beneath his feet. He saw the hinges on the pump-shed door glitter like hung decorations. He saw Rain leave the shade of his body and follow Hobbs into the pump shed, a fine dog. He saw C.D. Hobbs cover the last strides of his life like a herder who has more stragglers to round up. He recognized no choice other than the choice to stand steady, eyes open, eyes gathering, heart rising like a freed bird in his chest. It would come to him. The answer would surely come. He had only to wait and see how much of this destruction was his to share.

Acknowledgements

This novel arose from a story overheard at a potluck dinner in Laramie, Wyoming. I'm grateful to Jeanne Holland for telling that story with her usual panache. But the book found its true center as I traveled the back roads of Carbon and Sweetwater counties with Gary DeMarcay, who was then an archaeologist with the Bureau of Land Management. I'm grateful to Gary for showing me that landscape in all its beauty and strangeness. I'm also grateful to the late Staige Blackford, editor of the *Virginia Quarterly Review,* who published the story "Snow, Ashes" in 2001.

Thank you also to my readers Kim Kafka, Beth Kephart, Janet Holmes, Alison Harkin, Mark Miller, and Mandy Hoy. The National Endowment for the Arts, the Wyoming Arts Council, and the Christopher Isherwood Foundation all provided financial support. Sharon Dynak and the Ucross Foundation gave me safe harbor when I needed it most. Carol Bowers and the excellent staff at the American Heritage Center located the documents and photographs I craved. David Romtvedt and Simon Iberlin helped me with the Basque phrases. Bob Townsend of the *Owen Wister Review* and Dan Wickett of the Emerging Writers Network graciously published excerpts from the manuscript.

Bob Southard talked me through dozens of drafts. He is a dream critic.

Gail Hochman stayed committed to the manuscript. Katie Dublinski, Anne Czarniecki, Fiona McCrae, and the staff at Graywolf Press were patient and passionate. I consider myself very lucky to work with such wise and far-seeing professionals.

Finally, this book is dedicated in no small part to soldiers lost and found. It was written about war during a time of war. I remain humbled by the stories carried home by those who have fought in uniform.

Notes

The epigraph is from James Galvin's poem "Hermits."

Buren Adams's quotations in Part I are from Gilbert Murry's translation of Euripides' *Medea* and F. Storr's translation of Sophocles' *Electra*. His quotation in Part IV is from Thomas Fuller's *Gnomologia*. C. D. Hobbs's quotation in Part IV is a garbled version of a sentiment from Seneca's *Hercules Oetaeus*.

Many of the tales Hobbs tells in Korea are inspired by Lori Van Pelt's *Dreamers and Schemers: Profiles from Carbon County Wyoming's Past.*

I read many books about the Korean War. Eric M. Hammel's *Chosin: Heroic Ordeal of the Korean War* was both moving and influential. My descriptions of combat at Chosin are inspired by Hammel's account, but my characters and their actions are fictional. I hope curious readers will find their way to books by Hammel and others. The Forgotten War is not forgotten.

ALYSON HAGY is the author of four additional works of fiction, including the story collection *Graveyard of the Atlantic* and the novel *Keeneland*. She lives in Laramie, Wyoming.

Snow, Ashes is typeset in Sabon, a typeface designed in the 1960s by Jan Tschichold, based on Garamond. Book design by Wendy Holdman. Composition at Prism Publishing Center. Manufactured by Friesens on acid-free paper.